TOP MAN WITH A GUN

A Western Story

LEWIS B. PATTEN

SAGEBRUSH
Large Print Westerns

First published in Great Britain by Muller
First published in the United States by Fawcett Gold Medal

Published in Large Print 2008 by ISIS Publishing Ltd.,
7 Centremead, Osney Mead, Oxford OX2 0ES
United Kingdom
by arrangement with
Golden West Literary Agency

British Library Cataloguing in Publication Data
Patten, Lewis B.
    Top man with a gun. – Large print ed. –
(Sagebrush western series)
    1. Western stories
    2. Large type books
    I. Title
    813.5'4 [F]

        ISBN 978–0–7531–8007–5 (hb)

Printed and bound in Great Britain by
T. J. International Ltd., Padstow, Cornwall

AUTHOR'S NOTE:

It is to be hoped that Western history enthusiasts will forgive liberties taken by the author with respect to the dates of the first of the great cattle drives. Quantrill's raid on Lawrence, Kansas, occurred in August of 1863, while the great cattle drives actually began in 1866 and the first drives to the new railhead at Abilene in 1867. In the interests of story continuity, however, several of these years have been telescoped together.

CHAPTER
ONE

It was a day like any August day in Eastern Kansas — sky that was blue and all but cloudless, hot sun, the lazily whispering Kaw River below the spot where Clayton Fox lay in the weeds staring up at the sky.

Clay was sixteen — nearly seventeen. But not old enough. Even with lying about his age, not old enough to enlist. Not old enough to fight. That light peach fuzz on his cheeks and chin always gave him away.

Restless and vaguely dissatisfied, he lay staring at the sky while his young mind dreamed. Nothing — no premonition — told him that tomorrow he would be older. Or that tomorrow he would want to die.

Behind him, across a vacant stretch of prairie, the town of Lawrence, Kansas, lay. This day was August 20, 1863. A day like any day.

While the sun settled toward the western plain, Clay thought of the lands, of the dark-skinned tribes it would shine upon after it had gone from here. Next to fighting in the war, going West was the thing he wanted most. And he was almost old enough for that.

He heard his sister Mary's voice floating out from the house at the edge of town. He answered no louder than necessary to make her think she'd heard him.

Then he got up and shuffled reluctantly through the weeds and deep, dry dust. He was barefooted, a bit threadbare, slouched and indolent but possessed an unconscious grace of movement for all of that.

His eyes were blue — like a robin's egg, his mother had always said. Like ice, though, when he got mad. But blue, and maybe a little gray, the gray of the sky on a day before a storm. The color of water dripping from icicles on the north side of the house in winter.

His hair was brown, long at his neck and above his ears, long in a shock above his eyes that had to be continually brushed aside. He had freckles on his sharp, straight nose, and his mouth was not yet fully formed.

Tall and stringy from growth he was, but big of knuckle and big of foot. Clay Fox would be a big man when he had his growth and had fulfilled with muscle and flesh the promise his bones held forth.

Lower and lower sank the sun, staining the high-lying clouds its flaming orange. A flame in the West — blood in the sky. What caused the tiny shiver that traveled unexpectedly along Clay's spine? What caused his flesh to crawl as though with a sudden chill?

The house was a two-story gabled affair in need of paint and repairs. But these times were hard, or so Pa said, what with the war and the failing crops and all. There was no money for paint or lumber, and sometimes the food was mighty doggoned plain.

At the end of Quincy Street just off Delaware stood the house. It had sheltered slaves, escaping from their masters in the South, as had many of the houses in Lawrence.

2

Clay entered the yard by the back gate, stopped at the pump and ducked his head and hands cursorily under the spout. He dried himself on a flour sack hanging beside the pump, rehanging it so that the dirt he had rubbed off on it wouldn't show.

He shuffled up the path to the house and entered, glancing at his father as he did, to gauge his father's mood.

David Fox was a tall, stern man with a clipped spade beard and eyes as blue as Clay's. Tonight he looked at Clay almost as though he didn't see him.

He was preoccupied, as he often was these days. Behind the brooding sternness of his eyes was worry and controlled, smoldering anger. David Fox hated slavery in the single-minded, almost fanatical way a man of God hates evil.

Clay slid into his chair at the table. His father said grace solemnly.

Mary served the food and Clay and his father ate. Afterward Mary sat down with them and ate also. The sky outside faded from flame to gray.

David Fox got up to leave. He put his hat squarely on his head, saying sparely, "Meeting. I've got to go." He smiled at Mary and let his smile linger briefly on Clay.

The smile took the sternness out of his face. He said, "Help your sister with the dishes."

"Yes, sir." Clay watched him go, striding across the lot that made a short cut between the back door and the street. He supposed his father was off to another anti-slavery meeting.

3

Clay's life was a relatively easy one. He had certain chores, but, as long as he did them, his father paid little attention to him.

Mary, a pretty girl of nineteen, began to pick up the dishes. Clay helped listlessly.

Mary's young man, Lance Norton, was off someplace with the Union Army. Mary got letters from him irregularly, and between times fretted herself with fear for his safety. It had been two months now since her last letter from Lance, and there was a little worried frown between her eyes that never quite disappeared.

Except for runaways passing through, the Abolitionist meetings Clay's father attended, and the young men who had joined the Army being gone, there was not much in Lawrence to show that a war was going on.

Outside, dusk faded and the black of night came down, relieved only slightly by the moon, low over the western horizon. Mary finished the dishes and went to her room to write Lance. Clay, lonely and vaguely dissatisfied, went out and sat on the splintery back steps.

Again an odd uneasiness stirred him. He stared out into the darkness, puzzling at it. Then he got up and wandered out to the street. A night like any night, and yet . . .

He shook himself visibly. He remembered that the buggy horse hadn't been watered or fed and returned through the lot to the stable behind the house.

It was peaceful inside. Quiet. Faint aromas of hay, horse, oiled leather and manure combined pleasantly.

Clay led the horse outside to the trough and waited while the animal drank. Waiting, he lifted his head, nostrils flared, and smelled the breeze blowing toward town from the river.

No different than any night. No sound of cannon or musket fire in the distance. No clouds to speak of. No heat lightning or faintly rumbling thunder on the horizons.

He was suddenly very much alone. His father was gone. Mary was busily writing in her room, visible through the curtains that stirred faintly in her window.

Clay put the horse away and forked hay into the manger for him. Then he went outside and closed the door.

For a while he prowled the yard, glancing occasionally up toward Mary's window. She finished, and he followed the light of the lamp she carried downstairs and out to the kitchen. She came out on the porch, leaving the lamp in the kitchen, and settled down on the steps where she sat hugging her knees disconsolately.

He couldn't see her face, but he knew the expression it held. Lonely. Somewhat desperate with worry and fear. It always looked that way when she finished writing to Lance.

In a gesture both awkward and wholly unexpected, he put out a hand and touched the smooth top of her head. "He's all right, Sis. He's all right and he'll be back."

Startled, she looked up, her face unreadable in the almost complete darkness. She didn't speak, but for an instant warmth flowed between them. Then she laughed shakily. "You're growing up, Clay. And I think I like the change."

Now he was embarrassed. He moved away, but not far, and just stood still, doing nothing, thinking nothing. At last Mary got to her feet. "Pa will be late. I'm going to bed, and you'd better do the same."

"Sure."

He watched her go in. Something prickled along his spine. He stared around at the shadows, aroused now and wondering. He wasn't one to imagine things, and he hadn't felt either fear or dread of the darkness for six or seven years. Not since he was small.

Suddenly and quickly he turned and went inside. For the first time in his life, he thought about locking the doors.

Others in Lawrence may have seen them sooner. But everyone, at least near the upper end of town, heard them at precisely the same time. In the first gray light of dawn they came riding in, entering the town from the vicinity of Adams and Delaware and cutting diagonally across to the corner of South Park, two blocks from Clayton Fox's home.

Scarcely had they entered the town when they were seen by an elderly man who had gone out to milk his cow. He started to run — to spread the alarm — and they shot him dead as he ran. These were the shots heard by Clayton Fox, by David Fox and by Mary so early that morning of August 21st.

Probably most of the people hearing the shots paid little attention. The Fourth of July was not far gone, and firecrackers were still heard every once in a while.

Clay, coming into the kitchen, picked up the milk pail and headed for the shed adjoining the stable where the milch cow was kept at night.

He hooked the stool with a foot and pulled it under him. He began to milk, and the sounds of the twin streams were tinny and loud as they hit the bare bottom of the pail.

It was peaceful and still here in the morning. But his head lifted as again he heard sharp, popping explosions, farther away this time and fainter.

He finished milking and carried the milk to the house. He set it down and wandered out to the street curiously.

He saw them then, crossing the intersection three blocks away. And for an instant his mind would not believe his eyes.

Even at this distance they were recognizable for what they were. Big floppy hats. Beards and faces darkened from the sun. The bright, vari-colored "guerrilla shirts" which were the only uniform they wore. And the guns. Not one of them carried fewer than two revolvers. Some carried as many as eight, stuffed in their belts, in low-swung holsters, or hung from belts around their saddle horns.

Like a parade, they seemed to take hours to cross the intersection. Trotting their horses, they swept along like a tide, like a dark and dangerous wave.

A name came to Clay's mind, a legendary name, one both hated and feared. Quantrill. Quantrill and his Missouri Bushrangers.

Clay whirled to run for the house. And as he did, he saw the lead horseman of the six-man patrol round the corner at a hard gallop less than a hundred yards away.

Clay yelled, "Pa! Look out!" for something, some deep wisdom, told him they had not come this way by accident. This was the last house at the end of the street. If they were headed this way it could only mean they were after David Fox.

Fifty feet to the door, the thundering patrol fifty yards behind. Their revolvers began crashing, sounding almost muted because of the light charges of powder used by the guerrillas. They had learned that a lightly loaded revolver was more accurate than a heavily loaded one, but would kill just as effectively at short range. And powder was scarce in the South.

Something struck Clay in the shoulder, its impact like that of a mule's hoof. He stumbled forward, falling. But his voice roared out, unexpectedly deep, "Pa! It's Quantrill! He's got a thousand —"

He was down, and one of the guerrillas, dismounting from a plunging, lathered horse not a yard from where he lay, slammed him in the head with a carbine stock rather than spend another bullet on him.

He lay still, his head but inches from the familiar, weathered porch steps. Blood, bright scarlet, as bright as the facing on the guerrilla leader's shirt, flowed from his wound, soaked through his shirt, and mingled with the cool dew on the green front lawn.

Two more horses plunged to a halt not a dozen feet away. The other three thundered around the side of the house to cover the back door.

Clay heard nothing. He scarcely seemed to breathe. They'd have killed him instantly had they realized that he still lived. But their minds were occupied with bigger game. The name of David Fox stood fourth on the list carried by William C. Quantrill. It was the time for David Fox to die.

CHAPTER
TWO

Consciousness returned to Clay slowly. His head was splitting and his mind fuzzed, as though he were waking from a nightmare. He had dreamed the things he thought had happened and soon would awake, safe in his own room.

He choked and began to cough. He rolled, coughing spasmodically, and struggled up to his hands and knees.

The reason for his coughing was immediately apparent. A pall of smoke hung over the town, forming in layers along the quiet streets, rising in tall pillars above the crackling fires consuming many of the houses he could see.

Inside his own house, the smoke was thick and black, but, even through its denseness, he could occasionally see a tongue of scarlet flame. And the sound — like the crackling of a thousand bonfires. Or was it the fires? He remembered the guerrillas suddenly, remembered all that had happened. Most of those popping sounds were guns. The slaughter was still going on.

The sun was well up now, well up in the morning sky. With something akin to panic, Clay fought to his feet and staggered around to the back of the house.

He stumbled in the door. The kitchen was also full of smoke, but as yet there were no flames in here.

He fell over something on the floor and went to his knees. Soft and yielding it was, and Clay knew even before he turned what it had to be. A body. Either that of his father or that of Mary.

He clawed toward it, coughing again and light-headed from loss of blood. A nightmare, this. A living nightmare that simply couldn't happen.

He turned and scrambled toward the body. Terror struck his heart. His father's shirt-front was a mass of clotting, scarlet blood. There was a small, blue hole in one side of his father's forehead. His eyes were open, staring, his mouth slack and partially open.

Clay got up. Shock had numbed him and he felt but little pain. His mind was clear now too. He could think of nothing but Mary. She was somewhere here. She had to be.

He went through the house, and his clothes caught fire in the parlor and had to be beaten out with his hands. Up the stairs and into each smoke-filled corner, searching, crying out.

Sometimes his voice was deep, as it had been when he called that last warning to David Fox. Sometimes it broke and wavered between his boyish voice and his new man's voice.

He found nothing, but the search went on until at last he was coughing so hard he thought he'd suffocate before he reached the air.

Clay rolled down the stairs with a resounding crash. He crawled to the back door, and once outside, gulped pure air until he thought he would lose consciousness again.

He returned, then, and laboriously dragged his father's body out the door.

Out to the stable, the wall of which was catching fire from the blaze set in the weeds by sparks from the house. Release the frantic, rearing horse. The cow was next. He turned her out and let her go, as the horse had gone, away toward the open, limitless horizon a hundred miles away.

Once more into the house, into the kitchen that was blazing now. He seized the double-barreled shotgun he had noticed previously lying on the floor close to where his father had been. Its barrel was almost too hot to touch, but he hung on stubbornly, wondering if it was hot enough to discharge.

His father had tried, and, realizing that, he had stirred a strong pride in Clay.

A town swarming with Quantrill's men. Little or no resistance. Running, searching, Clay went toward the center of town.

A face was hanging in his thoughts — a face above a gray guerrilla shirt faced with brilliant red. He'd remember those cold yellow eyes, that hawklike nose, that thin-lipped mouth beneath the beard for as long as he lived. The face belonged to the leader of the patrol that had killed David Fox.

It had been twisted when Clay saw it coming hard behind him. Twisted with excitement and the lust to kill. The eyes had burned like those of a puma in a cage, and the teeth had shown between the lips, stained and brown from tobacco, stained as the beard beneath was stained.

Clay froze behind a fence as three drunken guerrillas rode by. One was waving a brown bottle by the neck. His hands were red with blood.

Clay raised the gun, lowered it reluctantly as he realized they had ridden out of shotgun range. The gun was loaded with birdshot. It was the only kind of shot his father had.

The dead man had had time to load the gun and prime it, and that was all. No time to fire before the guerrillas came bursting into the house. No chance to fire then, for one of their balls had taken him squarely in the head.

Clay went on, stumbling in pain from his wound, but too dazed to realize he was wounded. The sleeve of his shirt was wet and stuck to his arm.

More shots from down toward the Ferry. A veritable fusillade of them. More of Quantrill's men, roaming, looting, killing as they went. Women screamed. Clay passed one hunched on a lawn over the body of her man, sobbing hysterically.

A tiny core of anger stirred in Clay Fox's mind. And as he ran, it grew.

But tempering the anger was fear for Mary. They must have taken her. And he'd better not be discovered or there'd be no help at all for her.

The fire was spreading through the town, from one house to the next, from one building to the next. Down in the business district where stores stood side by side, it raged unchecked, burning without hindrance from building to building.

And down here the guerrillas were thicker. There seemed to be hundreds of them. Everywhere Clay looked, he saw more.

No chance of getting through. He knew that now. They'd cut loose on him the instant they saw him with a gun in his hands.

He retreated reluctantly. Mary would not have gone this far. Not of her own free will. And if the guerrillas had her, there was no chance of reaching her anyway. Not yet.

He retraced his steps. Weakness was beginning to overcome him. He shuffled along as though in a daze. He stumbled often and sometimes fell. He forgot where he was, forgot Quantrill, the guerrillas, his father's death. But he never forgot he was searching, and he never forgot Mary, for whom he searched.

Out to the edge of town he went and stumbled on beyond. The river would stop him or turn him from his course, but he hadn't reached it yet.

The sounds from the town had dimmed. He swung his head and looked confusedly behind. It sounded exactly as it had a couple of months ago on the Fourth of July. Firecrackers popping. Only there was a difference. A column of smoke marked the town for all to see within a hundred miles. The town was dead, and that was the smoke from its funeral pyre.

He heard a soft, hysterical sobbing off a ways to his right and stumbled toward the sound, crashing through the high and drying weeds. He heard a shot and dropped, and after that the weeping stopped.

Clay crawled forward, the shotgun pushed before him. He crawled for what seemed like an hour. All was still as death save for the distant sounds of conflict in the town.

And then he saw her, lying still and inert in the weeds. He got to his feet and ran to her.

He saw the drying blood that had drenched her dress. He saw the gun, a Colt .44 that one of the raiders must have dropped, a few inches from her hand. He saw the ghastly pallor of her face.

But he saw as well that she still breathed, and he flung himself to the ground beside her.

Clay shook her shoulder gently, fearfully. He felt the flood of tears building behind his eyes. He felt the tight control he had kept of himself beginning to slip, to crumble, as an earthen dam crumbles before a flood.

Mary's eyes opened, dilated and strange with terror. They did not become quite rational when they saw his face so close, but some of the terror seemed to pass.

Her voice was stunned and her words faint and hysterical. "Clay! They shot him and I threw myself down to cover him and begged them not to shoot again. But they did. They pushed me aside and put their guns against his chest and shot, again and again. The blood —" She wiped her hands ineffectually against the front of her dress as though to wipe the blood away.

Clay choked, "Where you hurt? You tell me now! Where you hurt?"

"They didn't . . . I thought . . ." Her voice died.

Clay looked at the .44 lying by her hand. He saw the new, fresh blood beginning to seep through the old on Mary's dress. Something sick and angry and cold was born that instant in his heart.

Deranged and half out of her mind from seeing their father murdered, drenched with his blood, she had somehow gotten hold of one of the guerrillas' revolvers and had fled out here. She had heard Clay crashing through the weeds and, thinking he was one of the guerrillas coming for her, had shot herself.

If he'd only called out! God, if he'd only called her name! It was his fault she was dead.

Now, suddenly, his youth and the things he had endured combined to overcome him. Tightness choked his throat. A flood of tears welled up.

He put his head down on Mary's breast, still warm with her departed life. And completely lost control.

He sobbed like a child. His body shook violently. It was release from pent-up terror and sustained horror. His tears washed away some of it but not all. Part man, part boy, there was something of it all that stayed and would stay for as long as he lived. It was the cold, angry sickness born in him as he saw that bright, fresh blood seeping through the old on Mary's dress.

Something else stayed with him. A face. A face twisted with cruelty and passion, yellow of eye, thin-lipped, bearded, hawk-nosed. That was a face he would see again. That was a face that would stay in his thoughts until he had met the man who owned it and killed him dead.

Even now, hysterical and half out of his mind, Clay knew he could not exact revenge against Quantrill's whole command. But against that one he could and would. He would never forget until that one had paid for his crime.

CHAPTER
THREE

Quantrill left the town shortly after nine, after one of his pickets reported the approach of a column of Union troops. He gathered his drunken, sated, loot-loaded band, formed them facing South Park, wheeled and galloped out of town. He left behind a hundred and fifty murdered citizens and precious few of his own dead. He left behind a town burning, sacked and destroyed. And rode in triumph toward the Missouri line.

The sun marched indifferently across the sky. The air was clear, save for that rising column of smoke. The River Kaw whispered as it flowed along its gently sloping bed.

Wounded and weak, exhausted and sick, Clay Fox slept beside the still, dead body of Mary, out beyond the town.

Lawrence picked itself up and dazedly began the task of quenching the flames, of gathering and identifying the dead, of preparing them for Christian burial.

The day passed and the flames spent themselves at last. Now the fight was concentrated on saving what was left, on finding those missing, on beginning life anew.

A search party found Mary and Clay and at first thought they both were dead. But when they detected warmth in Clay, they carried him carefully back to town and took him to the house of Lance Norton's widowed mother, who put him to bed and gently dressed his wound.

After that, he lay unconscious for five full days, breathing fast and shallow, pale as the sheets upon which he lay.

He dreamed during those long five days. He relived, over and over, the attack, the horror of wanton murder, of burning, of his search for Mary, of finding her dying by her own hand.

Yet through it all, one thing was constant. A face hung in his dreams, background for them as the sky or a landscape forms a background for a painting. Gray shirt faced with red. Yellow eyes . . .

Sweating, he started up from such a dream near midnight on the twenty-sixth. He was all alone in an upstairs bedroom that was strange to him.

He was thirsty and ravenously hungry. He sat up, felt his head swim crazily as he did.

He fought it and stayed in an upright position until the spell of dizziness passed.

Then he got shakily to his feet, steadying himself on the tall brass post of the bed. From downstairs he dimly heard voices, a man's and a woman's softer one.

The man's voice was raised in anger. The woman's was placating and soft.

Clay walked to the door, eased it open and looked out into the hall. He advanced cautiously along the hall until he reached a landing from which he could see the room below.

Immediately, instantly, even though his back was turned, he recognized Lance Norton. Lance was facing his mother, his very stance eloquent of his anger. "I'm not going back, I tell you! From now on I'll look after what's mine myself. I was gone, and she needed me, and where was I?"

"She's dead, Lance, and nothing can bring her back."

"But I can get the man that killed her. I can do that if it takes me the rest of my life."

"Then go back. One man can't defeat Quantrill. The Union Army can."

"And what will they do to him? I think you know as well as I do. They'll accept his surrender and let him go."

"The Lord won't let him go, Lance."

"Nor will I."

Clay staggered to the head of the stairs. He started down. Some noise he made must have startled them, for both of them turned to look.

Mrs. Norton, a stout, short woman, immediately got up and hurried toward him. "Clay! You get right back into that bed. You're not strong enough —"

Clay continued stubbornly down the stairs. He had lost weight. His eyes were sunk deep in their sockets, but they burned steadily at Lance. "You deserted." It was a statement, not an accusation.

20

Anger touched Lance's face. "What if I did? If I'd been here . . ."

Clay said, brushing past Mrs. Norton on the stairs, "Pa couldn't help her. Neither could I. There were six of them and they came so quick . . ."

Lance crossed to him in three long strides. "Who were they? What did they look like?"

Mrs. Norton said hastily, "Clay doesn't know, Lance. He was shot. He was unconscious when they killed Mr. Fox."

Clay couldn't, for a moment, understand how she knew. He hadn't told her and nobody else had known. Then he realized that he had been unconscious for a long time. He must have talked while he'd been delirious.

He said, "One of them I'll know. I'll find him and I'll kill him."

His face was still, his voice almost expressionless as he spoke. They looked at him oddly, and not as one looks at a sixteen-year-old voicing an impossible threat.

Lance seized him by the shoulders, his fingers like claws, digging into Clay's wound. Clay felt his head swimming, felt his consciousness fade. But penetrating, even through the advancing fog, was Lance's voice, intense, almost savagely so. "What did he look like? Damn you, tell me before I shake your teeth loose!"

And Mrs. Norton's shocked voice saying, "Lance! Stop it! Clay is Mary's brother! He's hurt. He's been unconscious for five whole days!"

Unconsciousness came then, a blanket lowering over Clay's fading thoughts. He heard, or dreamed, that someone was knocking at the door. He heard voices and felt his face being sponged off with a wet cloth.

Arguing voices. He opened his eyes and saw a man in the uniform of the Union Army talking to Lance. He caught the tail end of the man's words. ". . . have to see your papers. More deserters every day, and I've got my orders plain enough."

Lance's voice saying, "I haven't got 'em on me. I'll have to go upstairs and get 'em."

"If you don't mind, I'll just come along." Suspiciously.

"And if I do mind?" This from Lance truculently.

"I'll just come anyhow."

Lance grumbled something and their figures blurred. Heavy steps upon the stairs. More angry voices, arguing — and then a shot.

Lance ran down the stairs, his revolver in his hand. Smoke curled up from its barrel.

Mrs. Norton, who had screamed, "Lance!" upon hearing the shot, now sank into a chair, her face white, her eyes staring and filled with horror.

Lance looked at her coldly. "He's dead. And I will be too if I don't get going fast."

He crossed to Clay. He picked up the pan with which his mother had sponged Clay's face. He flung the contents of it directly into Clay's face.

Consciousness returned fully and immediately to Clay. With it came instant anger.

Lance put his face close to Clay's. His eyes were hard, his mouth a thin, straight line. His words were clipped and harsh. "You were her brother, but there's only one damn thing I want from you — the description of that man. Tell me and I'll leave. Give me any trouble and I'll slap the livin' hell out of you."

Clay's eyes burned steadily into the angry ones confronting him. He didn't speak.

Lance slapped his face, hard. Clay's head flopped to one side.

Lance demanded, "Tell me, damn you! Tell me! What did he look like?"

Clay was thinking that Mary had loved this man and had intended to marry him. He was thinking that Lance was not himself, that he was crazy with grief.

He stared steadily into Lance's eyes. They were cold in color, like the granite headstones at the cemetery when a winter wind blows snow against them. They were cruel, as devoid of pity as the eyes of a rattling prairie snake.

Clay said evenly, "I can't remember."

For an instant he thought Lance would kill him. The revolver was still in Lance's hands. The wildness of balked fury was in Lance's eyes.

Lance fought a battle with himself and finally won. He holstered the gun. "Then by God you'll come along and point him out."

Clay didn't answer. Mrs. Norton was staring at her son as though he were some savage stranger. Her voice was a whisper, "What about *him*?" and looked in terror toward the stairs.

Lance said, "Give me an hour, Ma. Then you can notify the Army that he's here. They'll take him away. I haven't got the time."

Her mouth was trembling so that she could hardly speak. "I can't stay here with him."

"Then go visit the neighbors. Only give me an hour. Understand?"

She nodded dumbly. Lance looked at Clay. "I'll get you some clothes."

He ran up the stairs, taking them two and three at a time. Clay heard him rummaging through the closets. Mrs. Norton got up and walked like an old woman to a desk in the corner. From a drawer in it she took a Colt .44 Navy revolver. She brought it to Clay.

She didn't have to tell him where it had come from. It had blood, a dark brown stain, upon the grips and cylinder. She said in a shaken, husky voice, "I won't need this. But you may. Take it, Clay. And God be with you."

Clay mumbled embarrassedly, "Thanks, Mrs. Norton."

"Look after Lance. He's in terrible trouble now, but he's a good boy. Mary loved him, and I love him too."

"Sure. Sure. We'll be all right." Clay was thinking that he didn't have to go. There was still time to stagger to the door, open it and empty the revolver into the air. The shots would bring someone.

Yet he discovered that he wasn't really reluctant to go with Lance. There was nothing here for him. Lance was the closest thing he had to family now. Besides, it wouldn't be right to betray Lance to the Union Army, no matter what he'd done.

Lance returned with an armload of clothes. He dumped them into Clay's arms. "Get dressed. Hurry."

24

Clay put down the revolver. He began to pull the nightshirt over his head, noticing that Mrs. Norton turned her back. It struck him as being a bit ridiculous that she did. She had cared for him through five days of unconsciousness. But he appreciated her concern for his feelings when he saw his body, white, bony, hairless and emaciated.

Lance said, "I'll get the horses ready."

He went outside. Clay finished dressing laboriously. Mrs. Norton glanced around at him compassionately, as though she'd like to help. But she didn't move or speak.

Afterward, Clay stuffed the revolver into his belt and sank back into the chair, exhausted, wondering if he could lift himself onto a horse, let alone ride all night.

Damn Lance anyway. He could have bludgeoned that Union soldier. He hadn't had to kill him.

He heard a sound. Lance ran into the room, gun in hand. He pointed it at Clay. "Come on." His voice was an urgent whisper. "There's a patrol coming up the street."

Clay got to his feet. Mrs. Norton began to cry. Lance pushed Clay ahead of him, out through the kitchen, across the back porch and into the yard. "Can you mount?"

"I don't know."

Lance came up beside him in the darkness and boosted him astride. Then he mounted his own horse.

They could hear voices inside the house now, men's voices. And voices in the yard in front. Lance said, "Easy does it. Stay close behind."

He moved away toward the alley. Clay followed. But just as they reached it, the back door flung open. A stocky, uniformed figure stood silhouetted in the light. He bawled, "Hey! Who's that?"

Lance spurred his horse. Clay followed suit, hanging desperately to the pommel of the saddle.

Dimmer now, the voice bawled again, "It's him! He's gettin' away! Git after him boys!"

But Clay Fox had no time to think, no time to be afraid. Lance was leading him along a reckless, breakneck path, between sheds and the charred ruins of buildings, over fences, up alleys and down, and it was all he could do to follow and stay astride his horse.

CHAPTER
FOUR

For fifteen minutes they thundered through the town. At first their thunderous passage was noticeable, coming as it did on the heels of the silence and peacefulness of the evening.

But as time passed, as the hullabaloo increased, it became apparent to Clay that they were being taken, as often as not, for troopers pursuing the fugitives, which most of the people in town apparently believed were skulking members of Quantrill's band.

Out of the complete confusion and chaos within the town, Lance Norton led him at last onto the prairie, so utterly still.

Clay sagged forward over the withers of his horse. His feet, braced against the stirrups and his arms, encircling the horse's neck, were the only things that kept him from falling off.

The horse, Lance's spare which was accustomed to following the one Lance rode, needed no urging to stay caught up. So all Clay had to do was ride.

Once well clear of the town however, Lance hauled his own horse to a halt and queried, "You all right?"

Clay grunted assent. But the strain of the night had been too much. His wound had opened up and begun to bleed again. His head still reeled from the severe concussion he'd sustained. He was unbelievably thirsty and he couldn't remember what eating had been like. Five days he had lain in bed upstairs at Norton's house. Five days without eating, unless Lance's mother had been able to get him to swallow milk or broth or something.

He felt his hands relaxing on the horse's neck. He felt the stirrups slip from his feet.

Lance said, "All right then, let's go," and reined away.

Clay's mount took two steps and turned. And Clay slid off. He remembered hitting the ground and nothing more.

He regained consciousness lying in a pile of hay. The smell of the place told him it was a barn or stable. It was dark. He was alone.

For a few moments he lay staring up into the darkness, unmoving, while his mind remembered all that had gone before — waking to the sound of voices downstairs in the Norton house, the violence that had followed.

Lance must have abandoned him, he thought. Then, as he started to raise himself, he heard the creak of door hinges and Lance's voice calling softly, "Clay? You awake?"

Clay licked his lips and croaked an answer. A few moments later Lance was beside him, lifting him up, holding a tin pail filled with cool milk to his lips.

Clay drank greedily until Lance pulled the pail away. "Not so damn fast. You'll puke it all up."

Clay asked, "Where are we?"

"Farm. Three-four miles south of Lawrence."

"Where are you going? You're not going to Missouri?"

"Why not? That's where they are, ain't it?"

"They'll kill us both before we get across the border."

"Not if they know I'm a deserter. Not if they know I've killed a Union soldier."

"You're going to try and *join* Quantrill?"

Lance's voice was irritable. "How the hell do I know what I'm going to do? All I know is —"

He stopped suddenly, listening intently. "Somebody comin'."

Clay listened. At first he heard nothing, but after a few moments he heard the distant pound of galloping hoofs.

Lance disappeared from his side as silently as a ghost. After a moment, Clay heard the squeak of the door. He picked up the pail which Lance had put down and gulped the remaining milk. It hit the bottom of his stomach and lay there heavily. Nausea touched him, but he fought it determinedly, holding the milk down. He'd need it, and it wouldn't do him a damn bit of good if he threw it all up. Besides, he'd make so much noise doing it he was bound to be heard.

Here in the darkness he was suddenly very lonely and very scared. But he didn't regret coming along with Lance. Lance was someone to be with and talk to. Lance was, for the moment, security, replacing that formerly provided by his father and Mary. Besides that, he was in no real danger. He'd done nothing wrong. Even if the troopers caught Lance, they wouldn't hurt Clay.

He laid still, trembling a little, waiting.

The troopers thundered into the yard. It sounded to Clay as though there must be a dozen of them. They hailed the sleeping house.

Clay heard querulous voices from the house. The voice of the lieutenant commanding the troop saying, ". . . probably came this way. We figure they'll head for the Missouri line . . . got patrols thicker'n flies 'tween here an' there. I got to search your place, mister. If you like you can come along."

He heard Lance's urgent whisper from below. "Bury yourself in the hay. I'll be back when they're gone. If they find our horses . . ."

And then he was gone. Once more Clay was all alone.

He could feel the heavy bulk of the revolver Mrs. Norton had given him pressing against his belly. He stirred and burrowed into the hay carefully, making little more than a soft, rustling noise.

A long time passed, during which he heard nothing at all. The suspense of waiting increased, until it seemed he could lie still no longer, until it seemed he *had* to stick his head up and find out what was going on.

And then at last he heard the creak of the door hinges again. He heard heavy, muffled voices, and after a few moments, the tread of boots upon the floor of the loft not a dozen feet from where he lay. A man called down, "Nothin' up here, Sarge. Just hay." The footsteps came closer and one of the troopers kicked at the pile of hay burying Clay's concealed form.

The boot barely touched him in the ribs. He felt it, but it didn't hurt. Scared, he was remembering stories he had heard about searches of lofts and loose hay in wagons. Usually the searchers got pitchforks and jabbed them into the hay.

Well, if worst came to worst, he could yell out. He hadn't done anything. They wouldn't hurt him; they'd just take him back to Lawrence and ask him a lot of questions about Lance.

But no pitchforks were jabbed into the hay and soon he heard the footsteps retreating toward the ladder. After that he heard the door hinges squeak again. There was some muffled talk at the door which he didn't catch.

He waited a while longer, then heard the pound of hoofs as the patrol thundered away.

Carefully, knowing the farm family might still be up and around, he eased himself out of the hay. He stood up cautiously, brushing hay from his clothes, shaking it out of his hair.

He was surprised at how much better he felt. He was still ravenously hungry, but the milk had provided relief from hunger's sharpest pangs and had also relieved his thirst.

Lance would be out there somewhere, watching, waiting for the patrol to ride away. Seeing that they had, he'd be coming back.

Clay walked cautiously to the ladder, feeling his way in the almost utter darkness. He climbed down carefully, without making a sound. He went to the door, which was an inch or so ajar, and peered through the crack.

Lance would wait until the family had settled down again. Their dog was loose, but it had barked almost continually while the patrol was here, and was still barking. It was unlikely they'd pay much attention to it now.

Clay stood for a long time, staring out the door crack into the starry night. A cool breeze blew into his face, carrying with it the scent of sun-burned grass, of earth, of stable.

With a tightness in his throat, he remembered Mary that last night, sitting on the steps hugging her knees and talking about Lance. He remembered that awkward, gentle gesture he had shown her, realized how strange it was he should have done so that particular night when he seldom had before. He even remembered the smooth, clean-washed, silky way her hair had felt beneath his hand.

He felt tears burning behind his eyes and blinked angrily to hold them back.

Outside the stars laid a cold, clear light on the ground. Clay thought he saw something move.

He strained his eyes. For several moments he thought he had imagined it, and then he saw it again.

Down there beyond the corral — there *was* something moving. Something bulky and dark.

Lance and the horses, returning for him. It was time to go. He could save Lance the risk of coming all the way in by going out part of the way to meet him.

He pushed open the door cautiously. It opened almost six inches before it began to squeak. He stopped pushing abruptly when it did and stepped on through.

Movement on his right — but no time to react. A carbine muzzle jabbed savagely into his ribs, driving a grunt from him. Then a low whisper that held excited exultation. "Don't make a damn sound, kid. I don't want to shoot you, but I will if I have to."

Clay froze. Half turned, he swung his head and could make out the shadowy figure of a man in a Union forage cap.

He looked out across the yard. Lance, unsuspecting, was approaching, now less than fifty feet away. The small noise made by the barn door, the trooper's savage whisper — these things had gone unnoticed by Lance because of the noises the horses made.

Lance wouldn't be taken alive. He'd fight. Clay waited for the trooper's challenge. But it didn't come.

This close, Lance wouldn't have a chance. The trooper didn't intend him to. Before he could spot the trooper here in the shadow of the barn, the man would cut him down.

Clay yelled suddenly, "Lance! Look out!"

He whirled around. The trooper's gun was up — leveled.

Clay lunged at him, striking him just as the carbine discharged. Both he and the trooper tumbled to the ground. The trooper hung onto his carbine, trying to bring it to bear.

Clay swung, missed, swung again and this time felt his fist connect with the trooper's jaw. He wrenched the carbine from the stunned man's hands and scrambled away, crawling.

Lance had left the horses and now came on at a crouching run. Clay yelled, "I got his gun! Don't!"

A shot crashed out. A second and a third. Clay scrambled to his feet.

The trooper lay in a kind of curled-up crouch. One of Lance's bullets must have severed his windpipe, for his breath came out whistling, sometimes bubbling as blood flowed in to close the hole.

Clay's body was like ice. He said in a shocked, stunned voice, "I told you I had his gun. You didn't have to . . ."

Dazed, uncomprehending, he found himself praying silently that the last few minutes be taken back, that this awful thing be undone, that the man be whole and unhurt again.

He shouldn't have been here anyway. The patrol had ridden away. They must have left this one behind in case the fugitives showed up here. If Clay hadn't had his head buried in hay he'd have known it too. And avoided the man some way.

The whistling, bubbling noise stopped. The man lay completely still.

Lance hadn't had to kill him any more than he'd had to kill back there in Lawrence. But he had, even firing

34

two more shots than were necessary into the helpless man.

The dog, a small creature of indeterminate origin, had come racing across the yard at the first sound of gunfire. Now it tore at Clay's pants legs savagely, snarling, growling, leaping back and in again, nearly out of its mind with excitement.

Lance yelled, "Git your horse! Let's get out of here!"

A lamp went on in the kitchen of the house. Clay kicked at the dog, nearly upsetting himself. He ran out to one of the horses, seized the reins and tried to mount. The dog, snarling, snapped at his pants leg and hung on. Clay tried to pull his leg up but with the weight of the dog hanging to it, failed.

The door of the house opened and a man in a nightshirt stood framed in its light, shotgun in hand. He raised it and triggered one barrel blindly at the commotion in the yard.

Birdshot peppered both Lance and Clay and rattled against the barn wall behind them. Lance yelled, "For God's sake!"

Already mounted, he rode his horse around to the left side of Clay's. He fired once.

The dog yelped and dropped away, afterward lying still upon the ground. Clay mounted, reined the horse around and drummed on his ribs with his heels. The pair pounded out of the yard.

Lance led away to south, which Clay at first thought foolish inasmuch as it was certain the farmer would tell the returning patrol which direction they had taken. But a mile or so from the farm, Lance swung abruptly west, yelling back by way of explanation, "They'll be lookin' for us south and east of here. They won't find out we went west until morning, and by then we can be forty miles away. And don't squawk. They want you just as bad as they want me now."

Riding fifty feet behind the shadowy figure of Lance, Clay tried to close his mind to that. Like it or not, he was part of this killing. By warning Lance he had made himself part of it.

Now he too was an outlaw, a criminal. He would be hunted, hounded, until he was caught and hanged.

He didn't try to justify himself. He didn't reassure himself by thinking that he had owed it to Lance to warn him. For he knew neither the Army nor the law would take that view. He had been hiding, trespassing on that farm. By warning Lance he had made himself a party to the crime. Now he and Lance were tarred with the same brush, a thing Lance wouldn't let him forget.

He closed his eyes and tried to close his ears. But all he could see was that helpless trooper lying on the ground. And all he could hear was the whistling, horribly bubbling sound of the man's last dying breaths.

Pa was dead, and Mary was dead, and Clay's home was completely destroyed. In the space of a few hours he had become a hunted thing, a wild animal to be found and destroyed.

Lying lazily on the bank of the Kaw, hearing Mary's clear voice calling him to supper, smelling the grass and the hot, dusty earth now seemed like a faraway, impossible dream. And yet that had been less than a week ago.

Now all was changed — the course of his life was changed. He might live, but he would have to learn to live as the hunted live.

A feeling of bleak despair came over him. Death seemed preferable to the life that lay ahead.

And he was scared — more scared than he had ever been before in his life.

Wounded and sick and afraid, he was a man tonight. Where a week ago he had been only a growing boy.

CHAPTER
FIVE

For Clay, that ride was a nightmare. He never recalled more than bits and snatches of it. He remembered the first few miles, recalled the halt for water when Lance tied him on his horse.

After that he was mostly unconscious, save for short periods when he came to long enough to feel the jolting, interminable motion of the horse, and to realize where he was.

Dawn came, and they stopped to rest their weary mounts. Lance rubbed them down expertly, watered them, fed them a little grain and picketed them in a grassy draw to graze. Only then did he look to Clay, lying prone upon the ground where he had been put down.

There was grudging admiration in Lance's voice. "You saved my hide whether you know it or not. That guard there by the barn would of got me sure. I didn't see him and I wouldn't of seen him until he shot."

Clay closed his eyes. Images blurred in his feverish thoughts. There was Mary, and then there was the face of the guerrilla. Then those would fade and he'd see the soldier folding to the ground and hear his gurgling breath.

Lance said harshly, "I don't know whether you'll make it or not. But we're going on. I won't be caught and I won't be hanged."

Clay didn't speak. He only wet his lips with his tongue.

"I'll get some food. There's a farm just over the rise. I'll get us a chicken or some eggs or something."

Clay felt his head begin to whirl. He wanted desperately to answer Lance, to thank him, but he couldn't make the words come forth.

He heard Lance leave, his boots making soft, whispering sounds in the dry grass. He heard a burst of gunfire, later, far away, and still he couldn't move. After what seemed a long time but wasn't really, Lance returned, running, panting harshly as he ran.

Clay opened his eyes. Lance carried a sack.

He didn't want to think of the price Lance had paid for the sack. But he knew what the price had been as Lance lifted him to his horse and the breeze carried to his ears the distant, hysterical grieving of the widow Lance had left behind him on that farm.

They were no better than Quantrill now. Stealing and committing murder when they were caught. Lance would leave a trail of dead to blaze his way across the land. Or Clay would. There would be no stopping it, ever. They would kill to eat, and kill to avoid capture, and maybe sometime, sooner or later, kill because they had learned to like the killing for itself.

Maybe for Lance there was some excuse. The Union Army had taken him away from Lawrence, where he'd been born and raised. They'd told him to kill and had taught him how. As a soldier he'd killed men he'd never seen before, from whom he wanted nothing, against whom he held no grudge. Now he was killing for a reason — to save his life, to eat, to survive. Yet this was wrong and the other had been right.

And Clay. He shook his head dazedly.

Unconsciousness, brought on by weakness and the jolting movement of the horse, was welcome now. It stopped his thoughts. It blotted out the bleak despair that turned his waking thoughts so black.

All day they traveled, avoiding settlements and farms. At last they left civilization behind and started across the vast, grassed plain, broken sometimes by ragged, rocky bluffs. That night, when they halted to eat, they were a hundred miles west of Lawrence.

This night Clay rested, sleeping motionlessly, almost as though he were dead, his belly full for the first time since the raid. And all the next day he rested, for Lance, prowling in the dawn, had seen the tracks of unshod ponies and figured they belonged to a scouting party of Indians.

The following night, however, they went on, traveling in darkness, unsure of their destination, only caring that the miles were forming a barrier between themselves and the troops searching for them.

Clay, helped by his youth and his tremendous reservoir of vitality, was growing stronger now in spite of the grueling pace, in spite of his wound.

The gash on his head, put there by the carbine stock, was scabbed over solidly and beginning to itch.

The shoulder wound gave him trouble, for he was constantly moving his arms. Luckily, however, the wound was clean. The bullet had passed on through.

Days and nights blended in an unending procession until Clay stopped counting them. They were safe for the present, having left behind the pursuit.

Perhaps the search would stop. Perhaps the Army would write them off as dead. But he had to admit it wasn't likely. The Army never closed a case except at the end of a hangman's noose.

As the long days passed he found a strange mixture of gentleness and cruelty in Lance. Or perhaps there was no gentleness at all. Perhaps he mistook Lance's bow to necessity in caring for him for gentleness, when it wasn't that at all.

September passed, and October, and blizzards swirled occasionally across the plain, born in the distant blue line of mountains and sweeping with premature fury out across the eastern flat.

Sometimes Clay and Lance would stay holed up for days. They had no place to go and were in no hurry. There was game to be had for the taking. So far they had not seen a single Indian.

At one such place, in a grove of stunted trees on the bank of a nearly dry and sandy stream bed, they stayed two weeks. It was here that Lance began to train Clay for the life he knew lay ahead.

"You got two friends, me and that .44 you got stuffed in your belt. Trust the .44, but don't trust me. I might sell you out but that gun never will. Not if you learn to use it right."

"You mean shootin' it straight?"

"That an' gettin' it out in time. You ain't got a holster, so practice gettin' it out of where it is, right there in your belt. One thing I found out in the war — shootin' straight won't do you a damned bit of good if you're dead before you get the chance."

Clay knew Lance had all but forgotten Quantrill and the guerrilla whose description he'd wanted so badly at first. Lance was thinking of himself, now, of the life that lay ahead, of the men hunting him and of those he'd have to kill if he didn't want to hang.

But Clay still saw that image in his mind — gray guerrilla shirt faced with red, yellow eyes . . .

For that one he would learn. Someday when he was grown, when the war was over, he would be going back. He'd find the man some way. He'd face him and look on equal terms into those yellow, savage eyes. And he'd kill — for his father, for Mary, and also for himself.

So he began to use his days, and by using them gained strength, and purpose, and began to heal and strengthen faster for it.

First of all, he ground the protruding front sight of the gun away against a flat rock. It caught on his clothes and prevented a smooth and uniform draw.

After that he found a way to stuff the gun into his belt so that the grips were handy to clasp.

Finding that the gun tended to shift with movement, he devised a homemade, concealed holster for it out of a worn-out pair of saddlebags, an awl, and sinews from a buffalo calf.

The holster fit inside his belt. Greased with tallow and anchored to his belt, it provided an easily reached, unmoving nest for the heavy gun.

A gun at first without loads. Before Clay ever fired it, he had drawn it a thousand times — two thousand — he didn't know. He began to enjoy the feeling it gave him, to be able to stand empty handed and fill his hand with the gun in little more than half a second.

And now he began to practice drawing it cocked, although Lance told him he'd shoot himself in the leg if he kept it up.

He'd hook a thumb over the hammer before he ever touched the grips. The pressure of tightening his big-knuckled hand on the grips would bring the hammer back. Thus when he drew the gun it was already cocked and ready to fire the instant the barrel came in line.

They moved across the empty, rolling plain at last, heading toward the foot of the mountains where the town of Denver was.

On a plentiful diet of meat and nothing else, Clay had hardened and filled out. Not an ounce of him was fat. His muscles were stronger now, his body heavier.

And he was taller, too. Never shorter than Lance by more than an inch, he could now look Lance directly in the eye from equal height.

Both were ragged, and their horses were sore of foot. Lance and Clay had long hair, curling down around their necks and ears.

Lance's beard had grown and now was full and red around his jaws. He made no mention of it, of shaving it off. Clay figured he was keeping it mostly to change his appearance and hide his identity.

Clay had nothing with which to change his. He still had no whiskers on his face. But growth would make the change, and he realized this. All he needed was time.

Coming over a slight rise forty miles east of the mountains, they came abruptly upon a camp.

Lance halted immediately and Clay, following close behind, ranged up abreast.

Three horses were picketed down below. A fire was burning. Saddles and gear were strewn haphazardly around the fire.

Clay had spoken to no human being other than Lance for nearly two months. Seeing those strange, moving figures below now stirred in him a strong excitement. He started to spur his horse but Lance reached out and caught his horse's headstall. "Don't be a damn fool. We don't know who they are."

"What's it matter? They're white men. They're somebody to talk to."

"By God you'll never learn."

"They can tell us the quickest way to get to Denver."

Lance said disgustedly, "The trail can tell us that."

Clay stared at his companion. Nowadays you couldn't see much of Lance's face for the beard he wore. But you could see his eyes, and there was no warmth in them. You could see his mouth, a thin line that never smiled.

For an instant, Clay caught himself wondering what Mary had seen in Lance to make her love him so. There was no warmth. But perhaps he had been different then. Clay hadn't noticed.

Down below the three men had gathered before their tiny fire and stood motionless, staring up. Clay said, "Damn it, you do what you please. I'm going down. I ain't talked to nobody but you since we left home."

Lance stared at him until Clay became uncomfortable, but Clay's glance didn't waver. He suddenly felt vastly older than his years because he could understand that, through the things that had happened to him, Lance had acquired a vast distrust for the human race.

Clay found himself trying to understand. He had lost more than Lance had lost, because he had lost Mary and his father too. But then, he reasoned, Lance had been much closer to Mary than he, hard as that was for him to admit. Lance had loved her as a grown man loves a woman. He'd wanted her and needed her.

Lance suddenly and unexpectedly changed his mind. "All right. To hell with it. We'll go down."

He touched his horse's sides with his heels and the animal moved ahead. Clay rode slightly behind, apprehension touching him now.

Suppose they were recognized? Suppose news of what they had done had preceded them?

He realized immediately how unlikely that was. Five hundred miles of wilderness lay behind. There was no telegraph out here. The Union Army had more to worry about than a deserter, even one who had killed a soldier, and a sixteen-year-old boy.

He wondered, though, what had made Lance change his mind and turned his head to study Lance's face.

Lance rode easily, straight in his saddle the way a cavalryman rides. His eyes were narrowed and intent. There was tension in him, a lot of it, but it wasn't a thing that showed. Clay felt it.

Something cold seemed suddenly to lie against Clay's spine. A feeling of uneasiness touched him. He said quickly, "Never mind, Lance. Let's go around."

Lance didn't turn his head. He said softly, "Shut up. You was the one that wanted to go down and talk, not me. So let's go down and talk."

Clay swung his head to look at the men ahead. Not until now had he given any thought to how wild and savage he and Lance looked. But seeing the wild look of those ahead, he suddenly realized that he and Lance looked almost exactly the same.

Ragged, dirty, bearded, he could smell the strangers from a distance of twenty-five feet, probably only because their smell was slightly different from his and Lance's smell. Or maybe his nose was getting keen. On the plain a man learned to use all his senses more.

One was short, fat, his paunch tight against the front of his dirty shirt. The second was of medium height, with a fierce, lean face. The third . . .

Clay felt a touch of shock. This one was slender and not as dirty as the other two. A man's loose-fitting trousers and a baggy shirt failed entirely to hide the fact that this one was a girl.

He shifted his glance to Lance's face. Still the feeling of uneasiness lingered with him, increasing as he saw the strange expression in Lance's eyes.

They were hot and hungry, and they never left the girl.

CHAPTER
SIX

The fat one boomed, "Howdy. Headin' up Denver way?" He held a rifle negligently across his paunch, but Clay had a feeling it could be brought to bear and fired almost as fast as he could blink his eyes.

The other stood watchfully, his thumbs hooked in his belt. Inches away from his right hand hung a holstered gun, a small one which, though Clay didn't know it, was a Colt pocket pistol, caliber .31.

Lance didn't take his eyes from the girl. He nodded without speaking.

And now there was silence. Clay didn't know what to say. Lance was apparently waiting to be asked to dismount and join the three. The three were waiting for Lance and Clay to leave.

Clay looked at the girl. At first he had thought she was ugly, or at least plain, but now he realized it had been an erroneous impression, created by her baggy, dirty clothes, by her short-cropped hair beneath a man's nearly worn-out hat.

He saw her eyes, big and soft and brown, her mouth, full and trembling, her cheeks faintly hollow beneath high, prominent cheekbones and flushing under Lance's steady stare.

Clay heard his own voice saying, "Lance, quit it!" It was sharp with anger, curt with impatience.

Lance swung his head. His eyes were smoldering, and Clay realized in that instant that Lance had never been guided by any emotion other than self-interest since they'd left Lawrence.

He had cared for Clay because it was expedient to do so. At first because Clay had seen the guerrilla he wanted revenge against, later simply because he didn't want to be alone.

Lance swung his glance back to the fat man. "Your daughter or your wife?"

"His." The man tossed his head toward the lean-faced one, but he didn't specify which the girl was, his daughter or his wife, or if she was either one.

Clay said uneasily, "Lance, let's go."

"Lance, huh? Lance what?" This was the lean-faced one, speaking for the first time. His voice was like a file rasping against a horse's hoof.

"Lance will do. What do you hear about the war?"

"Heard Quantrill made a raid in Kansas. Killed five hundred men."

Clay said quickly, "It wasn't that —" He stopped abruptly and felt like a fool.

A gleam touched the fat man's eyes. "From Kansas, eh? Or maybe you two was with that murderin' bastard."

Lance said, "Shut up, Clay."

"Lance and Clay," the fat man mused. "Runnin' away, too, I'll bet. Runnin' away from what, boys?"

49

Lance was looking at the girl. "Part Indian, ain't she?"

Neither man answered. Lance swung off his horse. He said, "Give her a bath and she wouldn't be half bad." He took a step toward the girl who shrank away, sudden terror in her eyes.

The fat man's voice was a whip. "Don't touch her!"

Lance swung his head, grinning. "Why not? I ain't seen a woman for three months."

Clay swung down off his horse. He was beginning to like this situation less and less. The two strangers had separated. The fat one began easing to the left, the lean-faced one to the right. A suggestion of a grin began to spread over the fat man's face. He was looking now at Lance's two horses in much the same way Lance was looking at the girl.

And Clay felt caught — scared. He understood that he and Lance had ridden into what had turned out to be a trap, something that apparently hadn't penetrated to Lance's mind as yet, so intent was he upon his thoughts regarding the girl.

Lance was no better than the two, and Clay realized this too. Lance had ridden in, recognizing even at a distance that one of the party was a girl and wanting her — without caring who she was or what she was. He had intended taking her from the first, even if he had to kill to get her.

Clay suddenly wanted to run. He wanted to whirl and streak for the high grass a hundred yards away. But he knew he wouldn't get ten feet. The pair had him and

Lance between them now, and in another few moments the trouble was going to start.

What part the girl would play, he hadn't the faintest idea. She apparently had no weapon. Nor did she seem the kind to participate in a cold-blooded murder such as this pair obviously had in mind.

To Clay it suddenly seemed incredible. He shot a glance, first at the fat man, then at the lean-faced one. Their expressions confirmed his suspicions. They were a couple of hairy spiders and had been just waiting for something to walk into their trap. The girl may even have been bait, being one of the scarcest things on the plains.

The fat man said, "Jase, you reckon they's a reward out fer these two?"

"Might be, Phil. They're runnin', that's certain."

"Reckon we ought to take 'em in an' see?"

"Might not be too bad a idea, Phil."

Clay felt like a mouse being teased by a cat. He yelled, "Lance! Wake up! Can't you see what they're up to? They're goin' to kill us for our horses!"

Lance yanked his eyes from the girl. His face was flushed. His mouth was slightly open, and he was breathing hard.

It was a moment before comprehension dawned in his eyes. When it did, they grew cold and narrowed until they were the merest slits.

His voice was soft. "You watch that fat one, Clay. And back away."

The fat man's voice matched Lance's for softness. "Don't hurry off, boys. Mebbe we could make a trade.

Give us the horses an' whatever else you got, includin' them guns, an' we'll let you go."

So there it was. Clay had been right. It *had* been a trap, and he and Lance had blundered into it.

As they backed away, the pair sidestepped, keeping Clay and Lance almost exactly between them. The fat one was grinning cheerfully, but there was a deadly, unclean quality about his grin. The other one was cold, his face as expressionless as it had been when Clay and Lance had first ridden in.

The situation had its irony, which Clay could see even if Lance could not. Whether they liked admitting it or not, he and Lance had become predators, just like the pair confronting them. Perhaps they were not as open and brazen about it as yet, but it was just the same. Lance had recognized the girl as such from the top of the rise. The only reason he had consented to ride in here was because he intended to take her.

Now he was going to be paid off. He and Clay both were going to die.

Clay shot a glance at the girl. Her eyes were wide and scared and kind of sick as well. She had watched similar scenes before, thought Clay, and knew this one would end as all the others had.

She met his glance, her eyes entreating, even apologetic.

Clay had been scared back in Lawrence as the raiders swept in sight. But it had been a sudden thing, soon over. This was different. It seemed to drag. Minutes became hours.

All five were silent now. The only sounds were the slight shuffling that the fat man made with his feet and his faintly wheezing breath, the fidgeting sounds the horses made and the girl's plainly audible breathing.

Step by step, Clay and Lance backed. Step by step, the deadly pair kept themselves abreast.

They were sure, patient, unhurried. Like a cat which knows its prey cannot escape.

Lance's voice was high, and touched with panic. "The horses! Run for the horses, Clay!"

He tensed to run. Clay's voice, equally sharp but containing no panic, stopped him. "No! That's what they want. They'll pick us off."

"They will anyhow. They'll kill us, Clay!"

Clay felt older than his years, older than Lance. He knew he was afraid, for he had that familiar empty feeling in his belly. His body felt cold, his lungs compressed. He doubted if he could speak in a normal tone.

He resisted the impulse to swallow. No use letting them know how scared he was.

And yet, even with the fear that gnawed at him, he was still in full control of his thoughts. And, he hoped, in control of his actions too. Panic hadn't taken possession of him the way it had with Lance.

Lance stared at him briefly, unbelievingly. Clay saw grudging respect in his eyes, and something else that looked like, but couldn't be, fear of Clay himself.

And then Lance broke. He lunged for his horse, his hand streaking toward the gun at his side as he began to move.

From his own standpoint, it was the stupidest thing he could have done. Running, he could not possibly shoot accurately at either of the threatening pair. Yet they could shoot at him, and would, for even now their guns were coming up.

And Clay was left alone — to face them — to fight them after Lance was dead.

The fat man's rifle bellowed first, negligently held no higher than hip level, but pointed unerringly at Lance, and following his erratic course. Cold-blooded it was, like a man shooting a running rabbit. The fat man's face never lost its grin or changed in any way.

Lance seemed to stumble, then recovered, and took almost a dozen running, faltering steps before he fell. In the interval, the gaunt man's pistol popped like a firecracker.

Surprise touched Clay. The .44 was in his hand though he did not remember seizing it. It swung toward the fat man, firing the instant the muzzle dropped into line.

Twice it fired and then Clay swung, dropping, to face the gaunt-faced one, who was handicapped by a range excessive for the caliber of his gun.

This time Clay raised the gun, pointed it, and fired just as the gaunt man did.

Pierced through the throat by Clay's bullet, the gaunt one dropped, gurgling just as the soldier back in Kansas had. Clay felt a shudder of revulsion run through his body.

All was silent behind him. He looked around, from the ground, but tensed to roll or rise.

54

The fat man was sitting down, like a carven figure from China which Clay had once seen in a Lawrence shop window. The smile was still on his face, but it had a ghastly, ghoulish quality to it now.

The rifle rested across his ample lap, against his paunch. He looked like a man on guard, sitting comfortably on the ground, a smile on his lips as his thoughts took an amusing turn. Only there was a difference here. This man was dead.

The gurgling behind Clay stopped as the gaunt one breathed his last. Lance lay on his face, stretched out, halfway between Clay and their two horses standing nervously, ground-tied with their eyes rolling and their ears laid back.

Clay shoved the .44 into the belt holster and walked to Lance apprehensively. He had never felt more alone in his life, not even back there in Lawrence after the raid. Around him for hundreds of miles there was nothing but wilderness, wild and uncharted and unfamiliar, with which he was wholly untrained to cope.

He didn't even look at the girl. Only at Lance.

There was no movement of breathing in Lance. Clay turned him over almost roughly and looked down into his face.

Lance's eyes were open, staring. He suddenly looked like a stranger to Clay. This was a different Lance from the one he'd known before the war, the one to whom Mary had been engaged.

This man was a savage, dead now, but savage still, made so by the pressures living had placed upon him. This was a man that Clay had never really known.

55

And Clay knew something else in that briefest of instants. Had not Lance been killed today, the time would have come when Clay would have killed him, would have had to kill him.

He was glad, as he turned and stared at the girl, that it had never come to that and that now it never would.

CHAPTER
SEVEN

Sixteen — but a man already, because he had to be. Older than that day in August before the raid. Older than the night he'd left with Lance.

And yet, enough of the boy remained in him to be shy as he looked at the girl, enough to be terrified at aloneness and responsibility and peril.

His voice was gruff as he gestured with his head toward the gaunt one's body. "Your pa?"

She shook her head dumbly, those great, dark eyes fixed steadily on his face. Clay cleared his throat. "Husband?"

Again she shook her head.

"How old are you?" He could feel the vague stirring of anger because it was becoming apparent what she was. Just a woman traveling with two men, being used by them, probably being sold by them, too. It made him a little sick to think of it.

"Fifteen."

"What's your name?"

"Dolly."

After that there seemed to be nothing to say. He stood staring at her. She stared back, her face beginning to flush slightly under his steady scrutiny. It was Clay who finally looked away. He scuffled his feet and said harshly, "Well, don't just stand there. Pack up your stuff. We can't stay here."

With those words he assumed responsibility for her. He also felt less alone. He had lost Lance, but he had someone still. He had this girl.

She went about her tasks competently, with bowed head, as though used to this.

And the full, heavy weight of the responsibility he had assumed descended on Clay. Now he had to decide where they would go and how they were going to get there alive.

Denver lay twenty or thirty miles to the west. But if he went to Denver, which the dead pair and the girl had only recently left, there were bound to be a lot of questions asked. Some busybody, alarmed at the thought of a boy and girl wandering around alone in the wilderness, was bound to write Lawrence. When they did that, the Army would be after Clay again.

The east was closed to him for the same reason. And the mountains beyond Denver were trackless and wild and teeming with hostile Indians.

South was also trackless and inhabited by hostile tribes. So was the north. It boiled down, he realized, to a choice between dangers. Go east and face hanging for complicity in the killing of that soldier, or go in some other direction and face death at the hands of the Indians, or cold and starvation, which were worse.

The girl had finished packing the horses and now stood docilely holding their reins, waiting. Every now and then she glanced at him covertly, but mostly she kept her eyes downcast.

Clay said, "You got any folks?"

She shook her head.

"Where you from? Where's your home?"

She gestured toward the east, her face assuming an odd expression that might have been hatred.

"Want to go back?"

Her eyes smoldered now. She shook her head violently.

"Damn it, can't you talk?"

She nodded.

"Well, talk then! Quit shakin' your head!"

"All right." Her voice was low and soft and a little husky, as though she didn't use it much.

"That's better." He felt mean for having spoken sharply to her. "Where do you want to go?"

She glanced at the bodies on the ground. "Away from here," she said.

"It's almost dark. Maybe . . ."

She kept her eyes steadily on his face, pleading silently. Clay said impatiently, "All right. All right! Only I ought to bury Lance."

Dolly didn't speak. It was lack of a shovel that finally decided Clay. He couldn't dig a grave with a knife and that was all they had. Besides, this was right on one of the main trails into Denver. Someone might come along at any time.

He walked to Lance's horse and started to mount, the reins of the other horse in his hand. Then he hesitated. Lance had been carrying a little money. He also had a gun, powder, lead and a bullet mold.

It didn't seem decent to rob the dead, but it wasn't smart to go off and leave things as valuable as that for someone else to find.

He dropped the reins of both horses and walked over to where Lance lay. He stooped and went through Lance's pockets. There was a leather pouch in one of them that was heavy with coins.

He stripped Lance's belt of the powder flask, bullet pouch and mold and took the revolver out of Lance's stiffening hand. A little shiver touched him as he did. Standing again, he looked at the other two. "How about them? They got anything you want?"

"No!" The word was angry, vehement.

"All right then. Let's go."

She mounted easily and smoothly, like a man. He noticed the way she had rigged her horses. The last one was haltered, the halter rope tied to the tail of the second one in line. She held the reins of this one in her hand.

Clay mounted Lance's horse, holding the reins of the one he had been riding. He led out without looking back, but he could hear Dolly coming along behind.

Five horses, a little money, a couple of guns and a few provisions. They could live, if they didn't run afoul of Indians.

For some unknown reason, Clay's mind was suddenly seeing his father. Almost as though he had wondered what his father's opinion of this would have been, he seemed to hear the words his father would have said. "It's neither decent, nor right, nor fair. You haven't got the right to risk her life and you can't take care of her."

But if he didn't, he would be alone again.

Scowling, he rode westward toward the distant line of mountains. The sun was setting, a ball of molten gold sliding behind the mountain range. Less than an hour had passed since he and Lance had stopped atop that rise to look at the camp below. Now three men lay dead back there, and Clay . . .

He swung his head and looked at the girl. She was apparently unworried; her face was composed. Her eyes rested on Clay, the expression they held troubling because he could not quite fathom it.

He rode steadily west until the last faint gray of dusk had faded into night. Then he drew in and swung to the ground. "We'd better camp," he said, "and make up our minds what we're going to do."

Dolly dismounted without speaking and again went competently about tasks connected with making camp. First she unsaddled all three of her horses. Then she led the animals out away from the campsite where she picketed one and hobbled the other two.

Clay followed suit. He and Lance had always picketed both horses but he could see now that there was no need for it. The hobbled ones would not wander far so long as one of their number was left behind.

However, since he had no hobbles, he picketed both his horses just as he always had.

Silently Dolly began to gather wood for a fire. She stopped immediately when Clay said, "No fire."

After that she unpacked some cold meat and stale biscuits from one of the saddlebags and brought him a canteen half full of water.

They ate in silence. Clay's mind was in a turmoil. He supposed the law would be looking for him for killing those two back there. They'd probably go easy on him because of his age, at least until they found out about the soldier. After that — he thought about being shut up in prison, day after day, year after year, and a feeling of hopelessness came over him.

If he didn't have this girl, maybe he could go over into the mountains, to the gold camps, and get a job someplace. There wasn't much law in the gold camps, or so he had heard. But he did have the girl and he couldn't just leave her here.

He asked, "What do *you* want to do? I can't keep you. But maybe with the money I got and what all these horses will bring, you could pay your fare back home."

She shook her head violently in the darkness.

"Damn it, I can't keep you! We, well, where the hell can we go that people won't get nosey?"

"You could say I was your sister. You could say we were coming to the gold camps with our father and mother. You could say they were attacked by Indians while you and I were out after the horses."

He scoffed, "And what about these saddles? And what about those three dead men back there?"

"We could get rid of the saddles."

Maybe it would work, he thought. Maybe he could get a job someplace in Denver. With what they had and what he could earn, they might be able to get along.

62

He finished eating, got his blankets from behind his saddle, wrapped himself in them and laid down on the ground.

The girl stood motionless in the darkness for a few moments, looking at him. Clay growled, "Good night."

Her voice was the merest whisper. "Good night." He had the impression she was crying, but he couldn't imagine why. He watched her as she got blankets from one of the saddles. She wrapped up in them, hesitated, then finally came and lay down close to Clay.

She was crying, softly and almost silently.

He said gruffly, "What's the matter now?"

"Nothing."

"Well, if it's nothing, what're you cryin' for?"

"I don't know."

"You cold?" For some reason a strange excitement leaped in Clay.

"No." And a vague disappointment touched him.

There was silence then, and at last her crying stopped.

But Clay didn't sleep. He lay there and stared at the stars and listened to the night noises apprehensively, his hand touching the smooth, cold grips of the gun in his belt. They'd use that thing about being brother and sister. It was the best chance they had — maybe the only chance they had.

He went to sleep and dreamed, and in his dreams every hand was against him. He relived the shooting of the soldier back in Kansas. He relived the shootings today. And went on from there into vague, unreal fantasies of terror in which he rode into a Denver that looked like a rebuilt Lawrence, Kansas, in his dream.

A mob met them at the outskirts and they were running, running, running, with the mob screaming in pursuit.

He woke, trembling violently and soaked with sweat. He had the feeling he had been yelling in his sleep, but when he looked toward Dolly he could not see that she had moved at all.

After that he lay still until morning, staring up at the stars that faded as dawn crept westward from the far, flat eastern horizon.

Decision came with the dawn, as inevitable as the coming of day itself. He wasn't a man, despite the fact that he had killed two men. He wasn't equipped to roam the wilderness with Dolly and keep her safe. He wasn't even equipped to keep himself safe.

There must be people in Denver like his own people back home who would take Dolly in and care for her. He would risk his own freedom by taking her there, but he saw no other alternative.

Once the decision was made he dozed and awakened to find the sun coming up over the horizon in the east, to find Dolly shaking him.

He threw back his blankets and got up. She brought him more cold biscuits, some cold meat, and the canteen. He ate quickly and without enjoyment.

Her steady regard bothered him and for some reason he was reluctant to tell her what he intended to do. She'd know soon enough. As soon as they got started, she'd know from the direction he took where he was going and what he intended to do.

Almost grouchily he went about the chores of breaking camp, of saddling the horses and getting ready to go. He wouldn't look at her as he mounted up. He guessed she knew then, for when he did glance at her, her face was lifeless and her eyes downcast.

He felt as guilty as though he had struck her. But then a kind of odd defiance began to rise in him.

She was a fool to have expected more than this. He owed her safe transportation to the nearest settlement and no more than that. He didn't owe her his freedom or his life.

CHAPTER
EIGHT

All day they traveled in virtual silence, Clay leading with Lance's two horses, Dolly bringing up the rear with her three. In later afternoon they came over a rise and could look down into the bustling streets of the growing, new town of Denver.

Its size was startling to Clay, who had expected no more than a collection of shacks and tents. He drew to a halt involuntarily and stared in amazement.

Everywhere, it seemed, new buildings were being built. Everywhere heavy wagons rolled ponderously in the streets, some drawn by oxen, some by horses or mules. Far in the distance, by the riverbank, was an Indian village.

And beyond were the mountains, capped with snow, blue and hazy with distance but stretching magnificently from the northern horizon to the southern one.

Looking at the town, Clay was more frightened than he had been yesterday when he and Lance had faced death at the hands of Dolly's two companions. But he wouldn't let her see, and so he said, "Come on. Let's get going."

He rode down into the streets, ignoring but very aware of the curious stares they got. Apprehension was building up in him, not allayed by any feeling of safety or any particular faith in the innate decency of those around him. He had seen what could happen within a law-abiding, peaceful town in Lawrence. He had watched Lance become an animal, interested only in the satisfaction of his needs. And the pair yesterday had certainly not behaved in a way designed to make him trust other humans.

On down toward the river he rode with Dolly following silently. He had gone less than half the distance through the town, however, when he saw a man walking along abreast of them, his eyes glued to Dolly, his expression a peculiar mixture of suspicion and curiosity.

He swung his head and knew instantly that Dolly had seen the man before. Her face was white; her eyes were frightened.

He slowed until she came abreast of him and then, as a heavy freight wagon rumbled past between them and the man, he asked, "Who is he?"

"A friend of Jase and Phil. He recognized me, Clay. What are we going to do?"

Clay scowled. The wagon passed, and he swung his head. The man was looking at the horses now, at those that had belonged to Jase and Phil. Clay stepped up the pace.

The man was almost running and panting hard. Clay touched his horse's sides with his heels and the animal broke into a brisk trot.

The man broke into a matching run, then stopped abruptly. Another heavy wagon rumbled past, loaded with logs. The distance between them increased.

Then Clay heard him shouting, and shortly thereafter heard the rapid pound of hoofs behind.

Panic touched him for the briefest instant. And cold fear. The man would accuse them of stealing horses and gear belonging to Jase and Phil. Even if they could disprove the charge, which was unlikely, they would be taken into custody and probably put in jail. In the meantime the bodies of Jase and Phil and Lance would be found.

He heard Dolly screaming behind him, "Run Clay! Run! Don't worry about me! Just get away!"

Pounding along, he stared back at her face. Her eyes were wide with fear, her face white. But there was something else as well, something he had never seen before and so did not fully comprehend. It was terror, not for herself but for him. It was sadness, longing, and fatalism, as though she had understood all along that nothing could come of this new relationship with him. It was resignation and a loss of hope. A few of these things he could feel even if he did not fully understand.

He dropped the reins of the horse he was leading and reined back his own. He cut between Dolly and the two she led, tearing the reins out of her hand and cutting the horses adrift. Then he gave her horse a vicious cut on the rump with the ends of his reins.

The animal plunged ahead, dodged another horseman and thundered up a side street. Clay swung over and followed.

Others had joined the chase without knowing why but caught up in the excitement of it. Now there were three horsemen less than a block behind the pair. The man who had started all this was nowhere to be seen. Clay knew why. That one was trying to catch the horses Clay had released. A grim smile of satisfaction touched Clay's mouth.

The sun was a ball of gold hanging suspended just above the jagged peaks to the west. An hour — if he could keep going for an hour, he could lose them in the dark.

They splashed across the creek at a hard run, the horses sending up great clouds of spray with their flying hoofs. Drenched, they climbed the bank on the far side, entered an alley, and shortly thereafter came out into another street leading east.

A couple of desultory shots banged out behind. Clay glanced back and saw that the original three had grown to six. But they were falling back, probably beginning to wonder now why they pursued at all.

With a little luck, Clay and Dolly would make it safely out of town. But when they had, what then? It was late fall. Winter was coming on. There wasn't another settlement for more than a hundred miles.

Today might be warm and clear. Tomorrow a blizzard could strike, burying the land in two feet of icy snow.

Clay's eyes were scared, but his jaw was firm. Dusk slowly settled down upon the land.

The pursuit slowed and finally stopped altogether as Clay and Dolly left the limits of the town and rode up a long rise toward the endless grassland that lay beyond.

He rode for yet another mile, then slowed and stopped his horse. The necks of both horses were gleaming with sweat, flecked with lather. Their sides heaved.

Clay got down and motioned for Dolly to follow suit. He loosened the cinches on both horses. He thought bleakly, Now what? and frowned down at Dolly's white and shaken face.

Their extra horses were gone and with them most of the blankets, powder and food they had carried. Gone too was the substance, the bargaining power the animals had represented.

It was nearly dark, but not yet too dark to see the expression on Dolly's face. Clay could detect but little fear there now that they were safely away from the pursuit. Only trust and dependence. Only confidence, taken for granted and therefore a calm and matter-of-fact thing with her.

It gave him a new feeling, one he had never experienced before. Until now he had been the dependent one, dependent on his father before the raid, on Lance after it.

It was a big thing, this new feeling. But enjoyment of it was tempered by the heavy weight of responsibility that necessarily accompanied it. He said gruffly, "Soon as the horses get rested up we'll go on. By morning we can be thirty-forty miles from here."

Dolly didn't speak, but her eyes never left his face. In complete darkness her face was now only a blur of white.

Clay waited ten or fifteen minutes more, every one of which he was acutely conscious of Dolly's presence so close to him. She didn't speak and she didn't move, but just stood waiting until he would tell her what to do.

He wondered what her life had been until now and felt anger touch him because he knew it had not been pleasant. Not as Mary's life had been before the raiders struck. Maybe, he thought, the sheltered and protected ones were those most hurt by life's cruelty. Maybe one like Dolly . . .

But he knew that line of thinking was all wrong too. Dolly wasn't hard. She was as vulnerable as Mary had been. She could be hurt as deeply and as easily as Mary.

He'd see to it that she wasn't, though. He'd see to that.

Because his thoughts about her were gentle, his voice sounded harsh in his ears as he said, "Time to go on. Mount up."

He swung to his saddle, waited an instant to be sure Dolly was settled. Then he led out toward the east, after first noting the location of the evening star in the west.

Alone. Alone on the plain teeming with hostile Indians. They must distrust everyone they met. They must avoid others of their own kind and depend on themselves alone. It was a sobering prospect and one which stirred a kind of quiet terror in Clay's heart.

Then his mouth firmed out and his jaw hardened. He'd do it because he had no choice. Hell, he hadn't done badly so far. He'd kept alive in that encounter with Dolly's predatory companions. He'd fished her out of the jam she was in. He'd avoided capture back there in Denver because he'd had sense enough to cut those extra horses loose.

The hours and the miles dropped endlessly away behind. When the sky began to turn dark gray, outlining the undulating horizon to the east, Clay pulled to a halt where a deep wash led north out of a wide, sandy stream bed and swung to the ground, saying hoarsely, "We'll hole up here for the day. Maybe later I'll be able to kill us somethin' to eat."

Dolly dismounted obediently and followed Clay up the wash, leading her horse. They picketed both animals and afterward Clay climbed to the lip of the wash and peered out across the lightening land.

He saw nothing. After a few moments he slid back down. "We'd better sleep a while," he said.

For the first time now, he noticed a strangeness in Dolly's eyes as she looked at him. A mixture of fright and resignation. He frowned at her perplexedly. He'd never understand.

But suddenly he did understand. And with his understanding came anger mixed with a curious kind of sadness. Because Dolly deserved more than her life had taught her to expect. She thought he was going to demand . . .

Her eyes downcast, she waited, trembling slightly.

Clay put a hand under her chin and raised her head. With the same odd tenderness he had displayed toward Mary that last night in Lawrence, he kissed Dolly lightly on the mouth. He said, "As long as you're with me you don't have to do anything you don't want to. Understand? I'm not Jase and I'm not Phil."

Tears sprang suddenly to her eyes and Clay's voice turned gruff. "Get your blankets and go to sleep. I'll watch for a while."

Her full mouth made a timid smile and she turned away. She went to where her saddle was and untied the small roll of blankets from behind it. She spread them out and lay down, afterward rolling herself up in them.

He climbed the bank of the wash and found a place to hunker down just below its lip. He stared out across the empty plain, moodily watching its changing colors as the sun came up. The future, their prospects for survival, stretched bleakly away before his eyes.

And he could feel her watching him even though his back was turned. Glancing around once, he caught a glimpse of her eyes before she closed them. Large, dark, they were as soft and vulnerable as those of a yearling doe.

CHAPTER
NINE

After that quick glance at Dolly, Clay kept his attention on the plain for a long, long time. Glancing back at her at last, he saw that she was sleeping.

Her face was relaxed, her breathing slow and even. She was curled up now, almost like a child.

He watched her, confused by the conflicting emotions running through his mind. There was irritation at having responsibility for her thrust upon him so unceremoniously. But there was gratitude, too, because she was company for him. Being alone now would have been more than he could stand.

She began to shiver in her sleep from the early morning chill. Clay slid down the bank, got his own blankets and spread them over her.

Her hair, short-cropped, was untidy. Her face was dirty. Her features were too irregular for perfect beauty, yet he found this quality appealing in itself. Her skin was dark from the sun, her teeth beneath her parted lips even and white.

Turning abruptly, he went back to his look-out post at the lip of the wash, frowning. He was remembering the way her lips had felt beneath his own and was angry with himself because he did. After that he didn't look at her. But he couldn't keep his thoughts from her.

The morning dragged past. Sunlight, beating down upon the land, warmed it in spite of the season. It was mid-November. Storms would be striking soon. What they would do if they were caught in a storm, Clay didn't know. They had no shelter and too few blankets. And he was afraid to risk a fire.

How many miles stretched between them and safety? It must be several hundred at least. He had traveled them with Lance and it had taken several months to come this far. But it had to take less than that going back. If it didn't, winter would be on them and they'd perish in the cold.

He found that all his reluctance to go back to Kansas was not because of his certainty that he'd be made to answer for the soldier's death. Clay shook his head irritably. He didn't like this unfamiliar confusion in his thoughts.

Movement upstream caught his eye, and he felt his body stiffen. His heart began to pound.

He saw nothing further, though he waited tensely for several minutes. Trouble was, the stream bed was hidden from him because of the bank of this wash. But he could see if he stood up.

Cautiously he eased out of the wash to the level ground above. Cautiously he raised to his feet, hoping he would see whatever it was that had attracted his attention before he was seen himself.

He did. It was a deer, a lone four-point buck, wandering aimlessly down the bed of the stream.

Clay dropped. If he eased down the wash, the buck would pass within a dozen yards of him. He wouldn't be seen until he shot.

But the sound of a shot carried, sometimes for miles. If there were Indians within earshot, they were sure to investigate.

Clay hesitated only a few seconds more. He had seen nothing all morning. Certainly the deer showed no signs of alarm, and he probably would have been acting nervous if there had been Indians nearby. Clay walked softly toward the bed of the stream along the bottom of the wash.

He stood at its mouth, motionless, waiting. Tension mounted in him. With most of their food supplies lost, it was important that he kill this buck. To have meat was worth the risk involved.

The deer ambled into view, less than twenty-five feet away. Clay drew his gun swiftly, thumbing back the hammer as he did. The deer leaped at the sound.

Clay's bullet caught the buck in mid-leap. Aimed at his neck, it struck the buck well in the shoulder. The animal pitched forward and lay on the ground quivering. Blood poured from the wound.

Drawing his pocket knife, Clay ran forward. Then he stopped and glanced warily around. He retreated at once to the shelter of the wash. There was no urgency about cutting the deer's throat. He was bleeding well from the wound.

He waited, his ears straining for sounds. He heard a faint rustling noise behind him as Dolly awoke and came down the wash to him. She came up close behind him, her eyes startled and wide from sudden awakening and whispered, "What is it, Clay?"

"A deer. I shot a deer. Now I'm waiting to see if anyone heard the shot."

He thought he heard something — very faint. He turned his head, listening intently. He took a step toward the bank and put an ear against the ground.

A rumbling sound — not loud — which meant to Clay the approach of several horsemen or buffalo spooking away from the sound of the shot. He continued to listen and the sound grew louder.

Horsemen then. If the sound had been made by buffalo it would have faded instead of grown.

Cold and sudden fear touched Clay. He had been a fool, he guessed, to kill that buck. He should have known better.

But he couldn't possibly have known. The chances of someone hearing a shot in this sparsely populated land had been less than a hundred to one. He had simply gambled and lost.

"Clay, what is it? Do you hear something?"

He nodded. "Horsemen. Two at least, maybe more. Don't make a sound."

He debated the wisdom of staying here. If he stayed, he took a chance of losing both horses because it was possible that the horses would be discovered first.

But if he retreated, he would lose what little chance there was of surprise. Whoever was approaching would first come to the place from which they had heard the shot.

Indians — it must be Indians. No white men would be traveling here. Clay couldn't help remembering all the tales of Indian atrocity he had heard. The tortures, the way they treated women captives.

He could hear the hoofbeats now without putting his ear to the ground. And could place the direction from which they came.

Quartering in from the northeast, from behind him. He should have retreated to the horses. Coming from that direction it was probable that they would find the horses first.

It was too late to move. He fixed his eyes on the grass above his head. It was blowing, bending north. Which meant the wind was from the south.

He heaved an inaudible sigh of relief. At least the intruders' horses would not smell Clay's and Dolly's. Nor would their two horses smell those of the intruders and give their location away.

Out in the open the buck lay, still twitching. Clay realized it had been scarcely more than a couple of minutes since he'd shot. And death was approaching on galloping hoofs.

Crouched against the bank, he waited breathlessly. Behind him Dolly was trembling. He glanced at her and tried to grin, but it was a dismal failure.

He was still a boy, for all that had happened. He was still almost paralyzed with fear whenever danger threatened him. He wondered if grown men felt this way. Some did and some didn't, he supposed.

Then for no immediately apparent reason, he began to get mad. All he and Dolly wanted was to cross the plain, get the hell out of the country. They threatened nobody and only wanted to be left alone.

The hoofbeats were closer, seeming to be almost over Clay's head. His hand, clutching his gun grips, was white at the knuckles and clammy with sweat. But his mouth was a thin, cold line. And his eyes were narrowed, hard.

Dust arose on his left as the Indians slid their ponies down the bank into the bed of the stream. Clay heard their voices, their guttural, indistinguishable words.

Die he might, and Dolly with him, but the Indians would not get off scot free. He waited, his knees trembling slightly, his body tense as a tight-wound spring.

They were hanging back, arguing among themselves. They had seen the deer and nothing else, but they knew that somewhere near the carcass of the deer was a man — a man with a gun.

At last they came into sight, sweeping at full gallop down the curving stream bed into Clay's view.

Four of them — more than he had thought. And maybe he hadn't seen them all. Maybe one or two had hung back to cover the other four.

Not much chance for Clay. Their eyes were questioning back and forth. The only cover was the mouth of the wash. The brave who saw him first raised a shrill, sharp bark of warning and started to raise his gun.

Swarthy faces, naked chests bronzed from the sun and gleaming with sweat and paint. Clay didn't know the significance of the different colors and patterns of paint, but he supposed that any paint meant war. It was what he had always heard.

Blue-black braids, a feather or two in the hair of each. Two spotted ponies, a bay and a black. Two were armed with guns, the other two with bows. His eyes took in these details, took in the lead brave's raising gun even as he raised his own.

His first bullet took the one who had yelled squarely in the chest. The man jerked violently and went backward over the rump of his startled, rearing horse. The others came on without slackening speed.

Clay's second bullet pierced the leg of the second brave in line, went on through and entered the belly of his horse. The animal went to his knees, got up again, whirled and ran downstream out of sight, the Indian sticking to his back like a cocklebur.

The remaining two whirled and raced out of sight. Clay's third shot missed.

One load was left. Only one. He had used one on the deer, three on the attacking braves. With hands that trembled violently, he snatched the powder flask from his belt and began to reload. Risky, he knew. They might sweep down on him at any instant. But the chances were that they wouldn't do that right away. They'd hold back now for a minute or two and talk things over. Maybe they'd try and take him from the rear.

He took time to reload only two of the empty chambers. Then he whirled. His eyes blazed down into Dolly's white, upturned face. "Run for the horses! Move!"

She broke into flight like a startled deer. Clay ran along behind, but part of his attention was on the terrain, the rest on the top of the wash ahead. He couldn't hear the Indians now at all. He didn't hear anything.

He didn't intend to flee. That would be fatal. Here, for a few moments yet, he had the advantage because he was hidden. The Indians would be exposed for the briefest instant before they discovered him.

Hoofbeats came suddenly from behind — hoofbeats that faded almost at once. He ran on, knowing they'd probably picked up their wounded companion.

Dolly reached the horses with Clay close behind. He whispered fiercely, "Get rid of those picket ropes! Get bridles on them! Then hold them both and wait!"

Almost beside herself with terror, she complied. Clay stood for a moment spread-legged in the bottom of the wash, his eyes roving back and forth along its lip.

Nothing happened. There was no sound. He climbed carefully up the bank. Slowly, warily, he poked his head above its rim. He saw nothing at first, but as he eased higher, he could see the rolling expanse of plain beyond the wash.

And he saw the Indians too. Riding away, both horses packing double. A third trotted along behind.

There had only been four after all. He breathed a sigh of relief and started to climb out. Then he stopped. Indians were clever and sly. What better ruse than to ride away, leaving behind one or two to pick him off when he showed himself?

So he waited again. The anger stirred by the arrival of the Indians began to grow. Damn them.

Clay slid to the bottom of the wash. He snatched the reins of his horse from Dolly's hand.

Mounting, he whirled the horse and pounded down the floor of the wash. He thundered into the open stream bed and turned left at a hard run.

Where the Indians had slid their horses down into the stream bed, Clay climbed out, and so reached the level of the plain. But nothing happened. There had been only four and they had gone.

More slowly, feeling weak with relief, Clay returned to the mouth of the wash where the deer still lay. He dismounted beside the carcass, and raised a yell for Dolly. After a few moments she came riding to him.

He dressed the deer, quartered it and propped the quarters in the shade of the bank. He washed his hands in the trickle of the stream. He said, "We can take about an hour to let that meat cool out. Then we've got to go. Those Indians will be back."

CHAPTER
TEN

With the meat distributed evenly behind both Clay's and Dolly's saddles, they rode out a little before noon.

Clay was aware that he had been lucky. He had driven off four toughened plains warriors. He had acquired enough meat to last them for weeks, provided the weather turned cold and it didn't spoil.

Right now it looked as though it might turn cold. A yellowish haze hid the western mountains, though the sun still shone brightly here.

He led, keeping to low ground and careful that neither of them were ever skylined at the top of a ridge. The Indians might return, but he wouldn't make it easy for them. They'd have to follow trail.

All day they rode steadily eastward. There were no trails here, but, from what Lance had said, Clay knew there were two main trails leading into Denver. One followed the Platte, lying to the north. The other followed the Smoky Hill River to the south.

Straight east was good enough for now. East, trail or not, would lead them to Kansas. If they traveled far enough and long enough they'd reach the edge of civilization with nothing but direction to guide them.

Toward late afternoon the yellow haze spread east until it partly hid the sun. The air began to chill and the wind, which had been from the south, veered until it was blowing steadily out of the northeast.

Clay didn't mention it to Dolly, but he knew they were in for a storm. A bad one from the ominous look of the sky.

Unconsciously he began to hurry the horses, even though he knew he couldn't outrun the storm. And as the sun sank in the western sky, he began to look for a place to hole up. Shelter from the wind was, he realized, of paramount importance. Here on the plains it swept unhindered for nearly a thousand miles. Shelter for the horses as well as for Dolly and himself. If anything happened to the horses they were doomed.

After that — firewood. Only there wasn't any firewood. A few snags and twisted limbs in the stream beds. An occasional stunted tree.

Out here you had to burn buffalo chips for both warmth and for cooking. So he must stop soon enough tonight to gather a plentiful supply before the darkness stopped the search.

There was a bluff in the distance, but too far to ride. Closer, nothing but gently rolling plain. Clay frowned. Another wash like the one they'd stopped in this morning was the only answer.

He stared at the land ahead. It raised gradually as it neared the foot of the bluff. Washouts were formed by floodwater running toward lower ground. He turned abruptly and headed directly toward the bluff.

The wind was icy now, blowing hard enough to whip the manes and tails of the horses. The sun had almost disappeared into the thin cloud layer to the west.

Clay watched a line that was born at the foot of the bluff. Growing out of a natural ravine, he was certain it was exactly the kind of deep wash he was searching for. Running from east to west, it would provide shelter from a strong north wind.

He was shivering now. Glancing behind, he saw that Dolly's face was blue with cold. Her teeth were chattering. Foreboding touched him. This was something they wouldn't escape. It was also something they couldn't fight. They could only endure and hope.

He reached the ravine at sundown and rode along its edge at a gallop, searching for a place deep enough to shelter them. He found it at last and, halting, swung to the ground. Over the rising howl of the wind he yelled, "Picket the horses in the bottom of the wash. Then come help me gather fuel."

Dolly took the reins of his horse, glancing worriedly at his face. Running, she dragged them down into the wash at a spot where the bank was caved away. Clay began to gather buffalo chips.

Armload after armload he gathered and flung down into the wash. Beneath some of them were dozens of black bugs. All were filled with holes that maggots had made when they were fresh.

Thank God for the buffalo. Tonight and during the next few days, Dolly's life and his own would depend on the fact that buffalo were plentiful on the plain.

Thank God, too, that he had killed the deer. At least they would eat.

Dolly climbed out of the wash and began to help. They worked steadily, swiftly, with almost frantic urgency, until they could no longer see the ground. Even then Clay continued to search. Scuffing his feet along the ground, fumbling with numb hands for the chips his feet dislodged. At last he gave it up and the two of them climbed down into the wash where the horses were.

Flakes of snow stung their faces as they did — icy flakes driven along on a screaming wind.

Clay kindled a fire with powdered buffalo chips and a little powder from his flask. He fed it just enough so that it warmed them. Not much danger of its being seen. No Indians would be roaming the plains tonight.

Dolly had a blackened fry pan behind her saddle. Clay got it and found three rocks large enough so that, placed at the edge of the fire, they would support it. Then he got a quarter of venison and hacked off some chunks with his pocket knife.

There was no water, but soon there would be snow. Already the air was full of it and it hissed as it sifted down onto the hot fry pan.

Eddies of air beneath the lip of the wash filled with the aroma of cooking meat. After a little while, huddled close to the tiny fire for warmth, Clay and Dolly ate.

The temperature had dropped alarmingly. It was so cold now that every breath seemed to freeze the membranes inside Clay's nose.

86

Bleak depression crept over his thoughts. He had been a fool to think he could get Dolly safely across the plains to Kansas. It would have been better to be arrested in Denver and thrown in jail than to perish in the snow.

Dolly got up and left the circle of firelight. After a few moments she returned, carrying both her own blankets and Clay's. She made up a single bed between the fire and the bank. She got into it. Her voice was low, scarcely audible, and she didn't look at Clay. "We can keep each other warm. But don't get to thinking just because . . ." she stopped, flushing painfully.

Clay built up the fire and piled buffalo chips near at hand so that he could replenish it during the night without getting up. Then he got under the blankets hesitantly.

Dolly lay rigidly at first. But at last, when he made no move toward her, she snuggled up against him and after a little while he began to get warm. He turned and put an arm around her. He kissed her cheek and found it wet with tears.

She tensed at the kiss. Then she began to shiver violently. "Are we going to die?"

His arm tightened around her. Almost as scared as she, he scoffed, "Naw. We'll be all right."

"I'm sorry I got you into this."

"You didn't get me into nothin'. It just happened, that's all."

He waited several moments. Her body was warm and soft against him. He felt older suddenly. He could feel desire stirring in him, but coupled with it were other conflicting emotions. What he wanted from Dolly was, he realized, something Lance had talked about and leered about, and wanting it made Clay feel guilty and somehow ashamed.

Another even stranger emotion restrained him. Dolly was his responsibility. If he didn't protect her, she had no protection. If he took what he wanted from her he would be no better than Phil or Jase or Lance. In Dolly's eyes or in his own.

For a long time she lay, strangely tense, in his arms. And then suddenly her body relaxed. Her breath was warm and sweet in his face and for an instant her lips were soft on his own. She sighed sleepily and closed her eyes. A moment later she was asleep.

Clay lay awake for a long time, the fires within him dying slowly. Then, holding her close against the icy cold of the night, he fell asleep himself.

He wakened, chilled and stiff, several times during the night and replenished the fire. He wondered if they would wake at all when morning came. Long before dawn crept over the snow-buried land, he could no longer sleep at all because of the cold.

Miserable and very scared, they remained in the wash for two days, staying mostly beneath the blankets to conserve their dwindling supply of fuel. At last, on the third morning, their fuel was gone and Clay knew that, live or die, they had to go on.

The horses were gaunt and lifeless. Clay packed the meat behind the saddles. He put Dolly into her saddle and wrapped her in blankets as best he could. He tied her reins to his saddle horn so that she would not have to hold them.

He could not remember ever having been warm. A permanent chill seemed to have crept into his body. Every movement hurt and his thoughts were bleak and despairing.

He knew now that they would surely die somewhere out on the screaming white plain before too long. But they would die here too. Only more slowly and without even hope to sustain them.

He rode up out of the wash into the deadly wind and a nightmare began for him and Dolly, a nightmare of cold, of misery, of fear and of doubt that they were even going east. All he had to go on was the bluff, and after that other landmarks spotted at intervals from the preceding one. Sometimes, because visibility was so bad, he had no landmarks to guide him.

Miraculously they made it through the day with no more than frostbitten hands and feet. Near nightfall, Clay found a place which the wind had scoured clear of snow and upon that bare place found a couple of arm-loads of buffalo chips.

Tonight, their minds were dulled. They huddled together apathetically with little interest in each other or in the certainty of their fate.

After that days blended together until Clay lost count. The storm went on and on, its fury unabated. Their horses weakened in spite of Clay's stopping wherever the wind had blown the ground bare enough to let them graze.

But the miles fell behind. Eventually the snow stopped falling and the wind abated. But the sun did not come out.

On the ninth day after the storm began, the inevitable happened. Clay's horse stumbled and fell and would not get up again.

Walking now. Walking, leading Dolly's horse. Stopping often to rest or to build a fire of buffalo chips in some sheltered spot. His powder was nearly gone, the meat frozen too hard to hack pieces off. Now the time of death was drawing near.

Both Clay and Dolly had become gaunt and emaciated. Clay fell often now. Dolly would simply watch him from the back of the horse when he did. Pity would touch her face, but she had not the strength to dismount, nor the strength to mount again even if she had.

The morning came at last when neither Clay or Dolly could get up. Unmoving, hovering between consciousness and unconsciousness, they lay wrapped in their blankets and waited for the end.

Late in the day — Clay thought he was dreaming at first — he heard sounds, voices, the slap of reins against leather chaps. He flung back the blankets and staggered to his feet.

He fell immediately and so crawled through the snow to the top of the bank behind which he and Dolly had lain.

Three men or horseback, three white men with half a dozen pack animals and spares. With a final burst of strength, he made it to his feet and waved his arms frantically. He shouted, but the sound was only a dismal croak.

But they saw him and stared in unbelieving surprise. Then, warily and with hands on their guns, they rode toward him in a group.

Clay collapsed into the snow. Though his consciousness faded, he could hear their voices and feel their hands as he was lifted and laid on a blanket beside the fire they kindled. They found Dolly and the single horse that was left. A few moments later Clay heard a shot.

Consciousness returned slowly. At first it was the delicious consciousness of warmth that he felt. Then he felt pain — in his feet, in his hands, in his ears. Struggling, he tried to get away from the fire.

A voice. "Hey! This one's comin' to, Frank!"

Clay sat up. He blinked at the three men standing over him. He said, "Dolly. Is she . . . ?"

"She's all right. Half starved. Half frozen. But all right. She'll make it and so will you."

Another voice. This one from the lips of the oldest of the three, short, squat, as broad across the shoulders as a bull. But a voice that was grave and not unkind. "What the hell you two doin' 'way out here alone anyhow?"

Clay's mind functioned sluggishly. He said, "Indians jumped our wagon. Dolly and me were out after the horses. We got away." He smelled something cooking over the fire and saliva began to flow in his mouth. "You got something to eat?"

The old one said, "Get him a plate, Luke. And a cup of coffee."

The third spoke while Luke ladled stew out of a blackened pot. "Hell, he's a lot stronger than he's makin' out. They ain't as bad off as they'd like to have us think. I say feed 'em an' leave 'em. Like as not they're part of that Jayhawk gang. If we take 'em along an' get jumped, these two will hit us from behind."

Luke gave Clay a tin plate and spoon and Clay shoveled stew into his mouth. He glanced over to where Dolly lay. She was still unconscious, but there was color in her face.

The old one asked, "Brother an' sister? Or what?"

Clay nodded dumbly.

"How long you been out here alone?"

Clay shook his head. He didn't know himself. It seemed like years.

Clay realized that he must have veered south, for all his determination to keep a straight course.

"Know where you are? Texas. North part."

The man said, "I'm Frank Goodwin. This here's my boy, Leonard. The other one's Luke Profitt, my foreman."

Clay felt a little sick at his stomach and slowed the rate at which he was eating. He chewed each mouthful deliberately and washed it down with a sip of scalding coffee. He finished, wondering if he would be able to keep the food in his stomach. The foreman, Luke Profitt, said, "Should've eaten slower. How long since you ate, anyhow?"

Clay shrugged. "Several days. The meat froze so hard I couldn't cut it." His voice was hoarse and croaking, not like his own.

Goodwin said, "We got extra horses. You two come along with us."

Clay nodded. He stood up, beginning to feel less sick and stronger. Leonard said quickly, "Look at that gun, Pa, an' the way he wears it. He ain't no lost kid that got away from Injuns. He's a —"

Goodwin said, "Shut up, Len. I don't care who they are, I ain't goin' to leave 'em."

Leonard said, "Bet she ain't his sister, either. They don't look the least damn bit alike."

Goodwin didn't speak this time. He just fixed his eyes on those of his son. After a few moments, Leonard grumbled something and looked away.

Goodwin said, "What do *you* think, Luke?"

Profitt, a lean, quiet-faced man with a gun hung low enough to show beneath his hip-length coat, said, "Same as you, Frank. You can't leave 'em, no matter who they are. I *have* heard of Jayhawkers plantin' people in the path of them they intend to hit, but I never heard of anyone plantin' half-froze, half-starved kids out in the middle of a blizzard. We can watch 'em anyhow."

Dolly was stirring, and the conversation stopped. But Clay felt a vast relief. He had accepted dying, but now he was going to live. Both he and Dolly were going to live.

CHAPTER
ELEVEN

Clay took an immediate liking to Profitt. Of medium height, Profitt was a spare, sharp-faced man with blue eyes that managed to be both penetrating and calm. He wore a sweeping mustache that was lightly touched with gray and stained with tobacco, a narrow-brimmed, uncreased hat, and high-heeled Texas boots. His spurs had great, Spanish cartwheel rowels and his gun seemed to Clay so much a part of him that he would probably have appeared undressed without it.

He moved with the same grace and economy of effort as a cat. He had a way of scanning the land around him ceaselessly but almost unnoticeably. Clay knew he never missed a thing — not an antelope on a distant hill, not a track in the ground over which he rode.

Though he was usually quiet-spoken, Leonard occasionally stirred him to clipped, short speech. When that happened, his steady eyes would harden. When they did, both Leonard and his father were likely to become abruptly quiet.

Leonard was quite the opposite. Arrogant, spoiled, he was as different from Profitt, indeed as different from his own father, as night from day. Neither soft nor

94

pampered, he was as lean and strong as Clay himself. There the resemblance ended.

From the first, Leonard looked at Clay with thinly veiled contempt — and at Dolly in the same way. Why he formed such a sudden and violent dislike to them both, Clay could not imagine. But he did not imagine the dislike. It was unmistakable.

They rested the remainder of the day at the spot where they had found Clay and Dolly while the two gorged themselves on hot food and slept in the life-giving warmth of the fire. But the following day they went on, with Clay and Dolly mounted on two of the spare horses they had along.

From talking to Profitt, Clay learned that Goodwin had delivered a herd of cattle to Abilene in late October and was now returning to his ranch in central Texas. From their references to Jayhawkers, Clay guessed that Goodwin was carrying a substantial sum of money, probably the receipts from the herd.

Goodwin rode away in the lead with Leonard following. Profitt brought up the rear. Clay and Dolly rode between Leonard and Profitt and occasionally Profitt would range up beside Clay to talk.

Miles and days dropped away behind, and, as they did, the snow on the ground grew thin and disappeared. The air grew warm.

Clay's strength increased rapidly, as did Dolly's, helped by plentiful food and abundant sleep. Three days after being found, Clay felt as strong as he ever had.

Dolly's returning strength was evidenced by a growing concern over her appearance. She took to brushing her hair with a horn-backed hairbrush Profitt had bought in Abilene for some Texas lady friend and given to her instead. She managed to find water someplace in which to wash or bathe each day.

Her clothes were more of a problem, but Profitt graciously solved that too. He gave her a bright-colored blouse which, though hidden usually beneath her short-length, ragged coat, managed to make her feel feminine again.

Every night before they camped, Profitt dropped back to scout the back trail. Though concern was not apparent in him, Clay realized that the danger from Jayhawkers seeking to rob Goodwin of the money he was carrying had not diminished with the miles.

He questioned Profitt about it and Profitt said, "They used to raid the herds, but they've mostly given that up. Now they wait 'til a man sells his beef. Easier. He's usually paid off his crew and instead of having to jump ten or a dozen men, they've only got to jump two or three. Cleaner too. They don't have to peddle any beef. And money ain't traceable the way cattle are." Apparently, however, he found no evidence that they were being pursued.

In spite of that, Leonard's suspicion of Clay did not diminish. His dislike became more pronounced and finally changed to open, vitriolic hatred. Clay didn't realize it, but it was Profitt's apparent liking for Clay that caused it. Leonard admired Profitt and wanted his

96

approval above all else. Yet all he ever got was Profitt's veiled contempt.

Clay avoided Dolly as much as he could, aware that their story of being brother and sister had to hold up if Goodwin's suspicions were not to be aroused. Yet he could not help watching her, watching the gentle line of her throat and cheek, watching the way her mouth curved so delightfully when she smiled.

Avoiding her, he missed the hurt that sometimes showed in her eyes, the puzzlement that accompanied it. But he did not miss the way she sometimes smiled at the others. Nor could he miss the look her smiles stirred in their eyes.

Leisurely traveling to save the footsore horses. Twenty miles a day, sometimes twenty-five. Five days and a little over a hundred miles from where they'd encountered Dolly and Clay, they camped early on the bank of a near-dry stream.

Dolly promptly disappeared downstream, carrying her scrap of soap, her ragged towel and her hairbrush. Clay began to gather buffalo chips and wood for a fire, after unsaddling and picketing his horse and hers. Profitt had dropped back to scout the trail.

Clay stared longingly in the direction Dolly had disappeared. He wanted to talk to her. He sensed that she was hurt at his avoidance of her. He wanted to explain.

Yet he faced a truth within himself that he had not been willing to face before. The things he felt for her were more than concern and a sense of responsibility.

He dreamed about her at night. He watched her endlessly on the trail. He was in love with her.

He glanced around. The elder Goodwin was busy building the fire. Leonard had disappeared, probably to gather fuel.

Suddenly, decisively, Clay left the campsite and headed down the stream.

Meeting this traveling trio had solved more than the problem of survival for Clay and for Dolly too. It meant that they had a place to go. It meant they did not have to return to Kansas, where trial and imprisonment awaited Clay even if he wasn't hanged, where nothing but mere physical safety awaited Dolly.

Now they could start over someplace in Texas. After Clay had found a job, they might even get married. No one but he and Dolly knew of the violence and death that lay behind. And neither of them would tell.

The winter sun was warm and the air was clear and crisp. The ground underfoot was damp from recently melted snow. Mice rustled in the drying grass.

But for Profitt's endless, wary scouting, it would not have been safe for anyone to leave the camp alone. Clay knew that had there been an Indian within miles, Profitt would have known.

He walked for about a quarter mile. An odd excitement rose in him. He hadn't talked to Dolly for days — not alone. During the storm they had been close, as close as two humans can be. But now. He had to tell her why he had been avoiding her. He had to tell her it hadn't been from choice.

That Leonard — damn him! First he'd looked at Dolly with the same contempt he'd shown Clay, the same dislike. But now. Several times it had been all Clay could do to keep from calling him on it. The only thing that stopped him was the knowledge that doing so might throw suspicion on his story that Dolly was his sister. If that part of the story was destroyed, the rest would be suspect too.

Suddenly he heard voices ahead — Dolly's and a man's.

He stopped. No chance to talk to her now. Leonard must be with her. Or Profitt was.

He turned to go back, obscurely angry and, he realized, jealous too. But he didn't go back, for his ears detected a note in Dolly's faint voice that worried him.

He turned again and silently hurried toward the voices.

Dolly's bare back was to him. She held the blouse in both hands, covering her breasts.

Leonard stood half a dozen feet away. His face was flushed, and his eyes were hot. He did not immediately see Clay because Dolly had his whole attention, but his voice carried clearly. "What you bein' so high an' mighty about, you damned little trollop? Clay ain't no more your brother than I am. You been sleepin' with him, so why not me?"

Clay's fists were clenched. Anger boiled up in him quickly, a scalding flood. This was different from the time back there in Kansas, in the farmhouse yard. This was different from the time he had killed Dolly's two murderous companions. This time he wanted to kill. He wanted the cold, smooth feel of his gun grips in his hand. He wanted the shock against his palm as it discharged. He wanted to see Leonard Goodwin go down.

His voice was hoarse and harsh. "Leonard!"

Leonard's eyes lifted. He looked beyond the girl at Clay. Dolly turned her head, her face pale, her eyes wide. Anger died quickly in her face, to be replaced by cold, new fear.

Her voice was shaky. "Clay, go back! It's all right. I can . . ."

Clay paced toward her. He felt wild — furiously angry, and reckless. Coming to grips with Leonard had been inevitable from the first. He was glad that it was now.

Had he stopped to think of it, the intensity of his own fury might have frightened him. And perhaps would have made him cautious.

He halted a dozen feet from Leonard. Leonard's eyes blazed with rage. Dolly backed until she was behind him and then hastily donned her blouse.

Her eyes were wide as she looked at Clay — wide and fearful. She was seeing him now as he had been that day facing Jase and Phil, the only difference being that this time he was not afraid.

He said harshly, "You've got a gun! Use the damn thing!"

No contempt now in Leonard's eyes. Clay said, "This way then, you son-of-a-bitch!" He stepped steadily, almost deliberately toward Goodwin. He came in range and swung.

100

Wild, unpracticed. The only experience he had fighting with his fists was that gained from fighting the other boys back home in Lawrence.

That violent right missed cleanly as Leonard stepped back. And because it missed, Clay went wild.

Whirled half around by the force of his swing, he now swung back, in time to catch one of Leonard's elbows in the mouth.

He kneed the man savagely, closing with him, hands clutching at Leonard's throat. He bore Leonard back, and down, and the force of their striking the ground tore loose his hands.

He smashed a fist into the middle of Leonard's face. Again and again. Leonard kneed him and pain shot up through his belly, doubling him. He rolled aside and Leonard snatched his gun, shoved its muzzle against Clay's side.

Clay twisted, elbowed the gun aside as it fired. He seized its muzzle in both hands, twisted, got the gun and flung it twenty feet away.

His fists thudded into Leonard's face, vicious, rocking the man each time they did, but they gave Clay no satisfaction now. He wanted more than this.

Again his hands closed on Leonard's throat. He banged Goodwin's head savagely against the ground.

Choking, gasping, Leonard's eyes burned up into his. Wild, afraid of the look he saw on Clay's twisted face. But defiance brought the gasping words to his drooling mouth, "She ain't . . . no sister . . . by God, she ain't!"

Clay released his throat to smash a hard, bony fist into his mouth. Lips gave and split beneath it, and teeth cracked.

But the words sobered Clay as nothing else could have done. They made him realize that he was fighting, not as a man whose sister has been molested, but as an enraged male whose woman has been stolen.

Sanity returned slowly to his mind. Leonard opened his bleeding mouth to speak again, and Clay cuffed him contemptuously across it with an open hand. "Shut it, or I'll shut it for you!"

He pushed away and got to his feet. Exhausted, panting, he looked dazedly at Dolly.

Profitt was standing beside her. There was an oddly mocking look in his quiet eyes. He said calmly, "Say, that was quite a thing!"

"Maybe you'd like —"

Profitt grinned. "Easy now. Easy."

Leonard got up. He glowered at all three, then turned and shuffled away toward camp.

Profitt said, "I'll be kind of sorry to see you leave."

Clay knew what he meant. After this, Goodwin certainly wouldn't let them continue with him. They'd be dropped off at the first settlement.

Clay didn't care. Dolly was through being bait.

Still grinning, Profitt said, "We'd better get on back to camp. There's six men on our trail."

It seemed to Clay that his grin had an edge to it. As though even Profitt were wondering now if Leonard had not been right.

He said, "If you're thinking . . ."

Profitt said shortly, "I ain't thinkin'." He walked over and picked up Leonard's gun. Then he picked up the reins of his horse. "Let's all go back," he said.

He walked ahead and Clay followed. Dolly walked beside him.

A kind of bitter discouragement touched Clay. Everything seemed to have changed for him the day of Quantrill's raid. He must have changed somehow himself.

Whatever the reason, violence and death seemed destined to travel with him everywhere he went. He felt a sudden, bleak certainty that he would never, as long as he lived, be able to put it behind.

CHAPTER
TWELVE

Profitt, when they reached the camp, brusquely took charge. His preparations were both unhesitating and thorough. Using buffalo chips and grass, the four men made up four dummies half a dozen yards from the fire, swathing them in blankets and placing saddles at their heads for pillows.

As he worked, Profitt explained. "Up until now, they've been satisfied to hang back where there wasn't no chance of me spottin' 'em. That was to throw us off guard. Now they're comin' close an' I figure they'll hit us tonight. Only we'll be ready."

Clay said, "They'll know there's five of us. They'll have found the place where you picked us up. The sign was plain enough."

Profitt looked at him approvingly, with some lessening of the reluctant suspicion in his eyes. He nodded. "I ain't forgot that. One of these beds will have a man in it — me — movin' around enough so they won't suspect it's a trap."

Leonard spat blood and spoke between puffy lips. "What about them two? Who's goin' to watch them?"

"You are. You and your father. You'll have 'em with you out there in the dark."

Clay glanced at Leonard. He didn't miss the faint thinning of Leonard's mouth, the slight narrowing of his eyes.

Goodwin had been watching his son and glancing occasionally at Clay. At last he said, "However this comes out, you two leave us at the first settlement we pass through."

Profitt said, "Hell now, that ain't right. The fight was Leonard's doin', not Clay's."

Goodwin stared at him. "I don't care whose doin' it was. I don't want nobody killed."

Openly sneering, Leonard stepped toward Clay. The light had faded now to the deep, gloomy gray of winter dusk. He said, "All right. Gimme your gun."

Clay stared at him coldly. He understood that thinning of Leonard's mouth, that narrowing of his eyes. Triumph had glinted from those narrowed eyes as Profitt had said both Clay and Dolly would be with Leonard and his father out there in the dark. Leonard meant to see to it that Clay caught a bullet during the fight. He wanted Clay's gun because he didn't mean to let Clay fight back.

Goodwin said irritably, "For Christ's sake, cut it out! Ain't we got enough to think about?"

Leonard whirled angrily to face his father. "Suppose he is one of them damn Jayhawkers? They'll be eight to our three, an' even with an ambush, we won't have much chance. Luke'll be right here by the fire where they can cut him down. This one will be with us, an' all he's got to do is yell out."

Profitt said, "Shut up."

"You can't —" Leonard's eyes blazed into Profitt's steady ones. After a moment they fell away and his face flushed dully.

Goodwin said, "Maybe —" He didn't finish.

Profitt switched his glance to his employer. He said, "Suppose he ain't one of 'em? You take his gun away an' he's just dead weight. He can't help us, that's certain."

"Do you think he's all right Luke?"

"I think he is."

"All right then, let him keep his gun. We'll damn soon know."

The sky was now completely dark. Stars winked in its velvet expanse. The only light was that thrown by the fire. Profitt said, "Get out away from the light of the fire. I'll build it up and sit here a while. And we wait."

Goodwin said, "Come on," and Clay followed him away from the firelight. Dolly, her eyes downcast, followed Clay. Leonard came after her, his face gray, his mouth compressed.

They walked for about a hundred yards. Twice Clay glanced back at Leonard. He couldn't see the man's expression any more, but he knew it had not changed.

Out here in the utter darkness it was eerie, but he could feel the menace of Leonard's presence and the fear that was in him because of what he intended to do. At the first sign of trouble, Leonard meant to murder him. And Clay had to see that he failed.

The familiar fear was with Clay again, but it was less this time — less than when he'd fought the Indians — less than when he'd killed Dolly's two companions. The realization did nothing to reassure him. It simply meant to Clay that he was becoming used to violence, hardened to it.

Goodwin said, "Spred out in a line. Girl, you get behind the rest of us. Lie down on the ground. And be quiet." He maneuvered it so that Clay was between him and his son, and after they were settled about ten feet apart, said softly, "We wait until Luke makes his move. Then we all cut loose." After a moment he added harshly, "We shoot to kill."

Leonard was on Clay's right. He rolled slightly until he was on his side facing the man. Leonard's first shot might be directed toward the fire, but Clay was willing to bet his second would be aimed at him. Not from the position Leonard now occupied, perhaps. There was too much chance of hitting his father from where he was.

Clay could afford to relax and wait until Leonard moved. When he did . . .

Profitt sat beside the fire, staring into its depths for a long, long time. Then he again replenished it, took off his hat and coat, sat down and removed his boots, and crawled into his bed. He lay still for a while, but occasionally he would stir as though uncomfortable.

Clay noticed that he kept his face toward the fire. He knew that beneath Profitt's blankets, his gun was in his hand. He was willing to bet that the man's rifle was within easy reach.

The tension out here in the darkness was almost tangible. No one thought of sleep. No one was drowsy, even as the hours passed.

First indication of the raiders' approach was a restless nicker from one of the picketed horses. Goodwin whispered, "Here they come."

After that there was utter silence for almost half an hour. Strain mounted intolerably in Clay. Leonard began to fidget restlessly. Goodwin sat stolidly cross-legged on the ground, his Henry repeater resting across his solid thighs.

Profitt stirred again, rolled, after a few moments turned restlessly back to face the fire. A small grin touched Clay's mouth. Profitt had scanned the shadows behind him. Satisfied that no one was approaching from that direction, he had turned back again. And yet, so far as appearances went, he was only a man turning restlessly in his sleep. The others appeared to be men sleeping deeply and easily, as many do.

Leonard alternated his attention between the fire and Clay, a few feet away from him. His hostility did not diminish. Dolly had made no sound at all. Occasionally Clay glanced over his shoulder to see if she was still there. Not that he thought she might leave, but he knew how frightened she was, helpless and without defense of any kind.

An elusive, shadowy movement at the rim of firelight caught Clay's eye. He stiffened, realizing suddenly how useless his revolver was at this range, in this kind of light. Leonard had a rifle and so did his father, but both would be as useless as Clay's revolver the instant the attackers retreated the short distance required to get out of the fire's light. That shadow he had seen had been less than a dozen yards from the fire. Yet it had been almost invisible.

Clay's muscles gathered. He eased to his knees. His voice was the merest whisper. "They're coming in. I saw —"

Gunfire crackled down there at the edge of firelight. Four of the sleeping shapes remained motionless, but one rolled violently, frantically for the cover of darkness.

Profitt was a sitting duck. The invaders had not come far enough into the light to be visible from where he was. Clay was on his feet, running.

Behind him Goodwin's Henry roared, though he could not have been shooting at a better target than a gun flash. And Leonard's larger bore, buffalo gun bawled.

The bullet sang an angry song close to Clay's head. He ran an irregular course, knowing he was silhouetted against the fire's light, knowing Leonard was trying to hit him.

At the edge of firelight, Profitt threw off the blankets and, still crouched, began to fire. The attackers' return fire was concentrated on Profitt alone. Clay knew he was hit when a leg went out from under him and he sprawled sideways on the ground.

Clay veered to the right, running as hard as he had ever run in his life. He came up behind the attacking six, putting them squarely between the fire and himself.

He hauled to a halt, panting hard from exertion. Profitt's revolver was empty and the man flung it on the ground. He levered the rifle as he rolled painfully into a prone position.

Clay thumbed back the hammer and took the man on the right. As though struck by a fist, the man staggered into the firelight. Profitt's first bullet spun him and knocked him down.

The remaining five whirled, backing involuntarily, backing the few feet needed to put them squarely in the fire's light. Clay followed, not aware in the excitement that doing so also put him in the light.

Out in the darkness, Leonard's buffalo gun bawled, followed almost instantly by Goodwin's Henry. Profitt's rifle roared again.

Two more men stumbled and fell, but one crawled frantically away, crabwise, until darkness enveloped him.

Three remained, one facing Profitt, two facing Clay. Their guns roared in unison, and Clay heard both bullets almost as one buzzing past to strike and ricochet behind him. His own gun bucked against his palm a second time and one of them staggered back and sat down, to be slammed sideways by a heavy slug from one of the rifles out there in the dark.

The two that were left whirled and ran, following the one who had crawled away. Clay started to follow, then stopped. Instead, he circled the fire, coming up on the dark, far side where Profitt was. He holstered his gun, put his hands beneath Profitt's arms and dragged him bodily back out of the light. The raiders had gone but that didn't mean they wouldn't take a couple of parting shots at anything they were able to see.

110

Clay released Profitt and squatted beside him, panting heavily. He heard the diminishing pound of hoofs out in the inky black of the night. He said, "Guess they're gone."

Profitt didn't speak. Clay said, "How bad you hit?"

"Leg. I don't know how bad. Help me over into the light."

Clay helped him to his feet. Together they staggered back into the fire's light.

He laid Profitt down. Goodwin and Leonard came in now, with Dolly close behind. Goodwin yanked a blanket off one of the dummies and spread it close to the fire. "Put him here."

Clay helped Profitt to the blanket. Profitt's face was sweating and twisted with pain. His pants leg was soaked.

Goodwin cut the pants away to uncover the wound. Clay left and went from one to another of the raiders on the ground, making sure that they were dead. Dolly poured water from a canteen into a pan and knelt beside the fire to heat it.

Clay stopped beside the third man and stared down into his face. For an instant some resemblance to someone known before. Why did memory of that bloody morning in Lawrence return this instant in all its vivid horror?

That face. He knew who it resembled now — the raider who had killed his father.

Savagely he seized the man and dragged him close to the fire. With that light shining into the bearded face, he stared long and hard. The clothes were different and the eyes were closed, but —

Clay was suddenly almost sick with hatred. As though touching a repulsive thing, he opened one of the eyes with a thumb and forefinger.

Blue — not yellow. A faded washed-out blue. This one could never look as cruelly savage as the one who had raided Lawrence. But those features.

He shook his head angrily, unaware that all four of the others were watching him. He turned his back on the body, shivering as though he were cold.

Profitt's eyes, though filled with pain, watched him thoughtfully. Dolly's face was frightened at the look on his face. Leonard seemed suspicious. And Goodwin, again busy with Profitt's wound, was frowning.

Luke said, "Clay, hell boy, they'd have cut me to pieces if it hadn't been for you. For a kid, you think mighty fast." There was a long moment's silence, after which Profitt said, "Mr. Goodwin, if you drop these two off at a settlement, I just guess I'll have to drop off too."

Goodwin grunted as he finished tying up the leg. He got up, wiping his hands on the legs of his pants. He stared thoughtfully at Clay. "Looks like you saved more skins than his. Want to work for me?"

Clay glanced at Dolly. Her eyes were smiling at him and proud. He turned back to Goodwin. "I'd like that, Mr. Goodwin. I'd like that fine."

He didn't look at Leonard. He didn't have to. Someday, sometime, he and Leonard would have to have it out. He hoped when that time came he wouldn't repay Goodwin's generosity by killing his son. For an instant a strange bleakness was in his thoughts, a strange kind of coldness in his spine. Then it was gone.

He and Dolly had a home at last. They had found a place in the world and were no longer all alone.

Best of all, for Clay, was the knowledge that they could stay together. And Dolly would be safe.

CHAPTER
THIRTEEN

They buried the three raiders, then let the fire die and went to sleep. Leonard took the first watch and Clay the second. Profitt tossed uncomfortably in his bed, sleeping very little.

His wound was a flesh wound, but it had bled considerably, leaving him weak and dizzy. As it closed and clotted, it hurt. Pain spread down to his ankle and all the way up to his hip. When he got up in the morning, his eyes were red, his disposition edgy.

But he would not rest and insisted that they go on. They had been too long on the trail already, he said.

They traveled slowly south, but in mid-afternoon Profitt was so weak they were forced to stop again.

Clay helped picket the horses, helped gather fuel and build the fire. Dolly took over the cooking as though she had always done it and, whenever she had a moment, tried to make Profitt more comfortable. Watching her, Clay felt an obscure stir of jealousy.

Leonard avoided them both ostentatiously, scowling whenever forced to come near either one.

Now that he was headed away from Kansas, Clay felt an elusive regret. His thirst for vengeance had been renewed by the resemblance the dead raider had borne to the one he hated so. He realized that by leaving Kansas, he was leaving behind all chance to exact the vengeance he thirsted for.

He promised himself that, one way or another, he would someday be coming back. He would search through Missouri and Kansas too, if need be, until he found the man.

Days slipped away as their course led ever south. They traveled even fewer miles each day than they had before, but because they did Profitt began to recover.

Mending, he watched Clay in a strange way and drew him into conversation whenever he could. Little by little, he wormed enough of Clay's real story out of him to destroy the story Clay had told the others.

On one such occasion, Profitt said, "Can't say I blame you for not trustin' other people much. But you'll find a few that you can trust. Dolly there — she's one. I'm another, though you may not believe it yet. Goodwin's a third. To show you just how much you've let slip to me —" He grinned at Clay mockingly. "You was in on that Quantrill raid. Your folks was killed. You pulled out an' came west with a deserter. Must've killed someone or neither of you would likely have run so far. You ain't let slip how you come to meet up with Dolly yet, or how you lost your deserter friend, but you will."

"The hell I will." Clay was more angry at himself for letting this much slip than with Profitt for catching it.

Profitt asked, "How old are you?"

"Seventeen."

"An' you've already killed two — three. How many?"

Clay scowled at him.

Profitt paid no attention. "No matter." His expression had sobered. He said, "Right now you got a choice to make. Either you wear a gun or you don't. If you wear it, you'll use it. You're that kind. If you don't wear it, you'll probably get killed."

Clay said, "I ain't goin' to give it up." He was thinking of the defenseless people in Lawrence who might have saved themselves if they all had carried guns. He was thinking of Dolly's two companions. Whoever had ridden into their camp without the means of defending themselves would have died even more quickly than Lance had died.

Profitt nodded almost regretfully. "I didn't figure you would. All right then. If you're goin' to keep it you'd better learn to use it."

Clay felt a touch of irritation and couldn't help saying, "I don't do so bad." Afterward he felt like a fool.

Profitt grinned. "First thing you got to learn is not to be ringy about how good you are. But you're right. You don't do too bad. Trouble is that ain't good enough. If you want to stay alive, you got to be as good as you can get and sometimes even then —"

Clay didn't say anything. After a moment, Profitt said, "Where we're goin' men wear guns. Most of 'em wear 'em for varmints and such or because everybody else does. But there's a few that carry their guns like a carpenter carries a tool — to use. When a man wears his gun that way, he gets plenty of chances to use it. And right now you're that kind. You got yourself a slick belt-draw holster. You shoot straight and your mind works whether you're scared or not."

116

He shifted position uncomfortably. "You can be better, faster, more accurate, if you want to be. Point is, do you want to be?"

Clay nodded. He was thinking of that raider, of his yellow, savage eyes, of the bright, blood-red facing on his guerrilla shirt.

"Why?"

Clay suddenly wanted to trust someone. He said, "I was in Lawrence when Quantrill raided it. They shot me and killed my pa. They drove my sister half out of her mind until she shot herself. Yeah. I want to be better than I am. I want to be good enough to kill the one that did it when I meet up with him. I don't want to shoot him in the back. I want to stand there face to face and tell him who I am. I want to tell him why I'm killing him before I do it."

There was a peculiar deadly intensity to his voice, in the expression on his face.

But Profitt nodded. "I guess I got no quarrel with that. All right. You won't save much time no matter how much you practice. Maybe a little part of a second here and there. But the difference between the fastest man in the world and the slowest is less'n a second anyhow."

Thereafter, whenever they had a chance, the pair would practice. Sometimes they would drop behind during the course of the day's travel and, hidden by the steep bank of a stream, fire at rocks and twigs in the bank itself. Sometimes they wouldn't fire at all, but would only practice drawing their guns.

Clay was surprised to learn that, even now, Profitt practiced continuously every day. "Like anything else," said Luke. "If you don't practice every day you get rusty and clumsy and slow. Then when your life maybe depends on bein' fast, you ain't. You're dead instead. Time'll come, maybe, when a man won't have to wear a gun at all. But it ain't come yet."

Clay did not, however, give up the belt holster. He had grown used to the snug way it fitted against his flat belly. And he found that, whatever position he was forced to draw from, the gun never shifted or moved like Profitt's did.

There came a morning when, crossing the seemingly endless plain, Profitt grinned at Clay and said, "We're home."

Clay stared at him perplexedly.

"This is Goodwin's Cross Bar Ranch. It starts here. Two more days of ridin' an' we'll reach the home place."

Occasionally now, they came upon little groups of cattle, great, vari-colored beasts that appeared to Clay to be all bony hips and legs.

Leonard remained withdrawn, a surly look habitually on his face. Goodwin occasionally stared at Clay as though wondering at the wisdom of hiring him. He plainly did not approve of Profitt's coaching, but he made no vocal protest.

On the evening of the second day, they sighted the ranch buildings in the distance.

Clay didn't know what he had expected. Certainly he had thought there would be trees — some growing crops perhaps. He was not prepared for what he saw.

It looked like a fort — adobe wall surrounding a sprawling adobe house with pole-supported galleries on two sides. Ugly, a house of mud, a wall of mud, with towers at each corner of the square formed by the ten-foot-high wall. And gates, huge, rough-hewn gates on heavy, rusted hinges.

Behind the walled enclosure more buildings — a hodgepodge of adobe and lumber, most of them roofed with sod. And adobe corrals that looked large enough to hold a thousand head.

People too, seemingly hundreds of then. Half naked Mexican children came running out to meet them, screeching and laughing. And the ride to the house with barefooted children screaming along in pursuit, dozens of dogs barking and quarreling, gaunt and hard-eyed men riding out to add to the confusion, yelling and firing their guns into the air.

And a woman, a woman like Clay had never seen before on the great, long gallery of the house.

They reined up, dusty, tired, and swung to the ground. Goodwin caught the woman on the gallery in his arms and hugged her. She kissed both Profitt and Leonard in turn. She stared long and hard at Dolly, then shifted her direct, penetrating glance to Clay.

She was tall for a woman, leggy as a colt in her split green riding skirt. Her hair was red, the color of a winter sunset and seemed to have a glowing light of its own. Piled and coiled carelessly on her head, Clay thought that, loosened, it must fall below her waist.

Her skin was dark from the sun but smooth. Her lips were full and red, gleaming as her tongue came out to moisten them.

The way she looked at Clay made him feel hotly uncomfortable. He stared down at his feet and his face got red. She laughed, a warm, mocking, pleasant sound that made Clay even more uncomfortable.

Vaguely angered, he looked up to meet her steady, probing eyes with a stare of his own, just as steady and angry too.

She wore a Mexican *camisa* above her riding skirt that carelessly revealed the rounded upper parts of her shoulders and breasts. Her teeth were white, as strong as Dolly's were. She said suddenly, "I'm Diana Goodwin."

Profitt said drily, "This is Clay Fox, Di. And his sister Dolly. We found 'em out on the prairie half froze from a storm. When you get through starin' at him like he was a prize stallion or something, you might see about finding a room for Dolly. Come on, Clay."

Clay turned away from Diana with mixed feelings of regret and relief. Something about her fascinated him but her boldly appraising stare embarrassed him. He wondered briefly at Profitt giving her orders, but she turned, smiling oddly, and took Dolly into the house with her. Clay glanced back over his shoulder and saw her watching him from the doorway.

He said, "Mr. Goodwin's wife?"

Profitt laughed shortly. "Nobody's wife. She's Goodwin's daughter. And between her an' Leonard, you got your work cut out for you."

Clay didn't question him as to what he meant by that remark. He was too busy staring around him at the workings of the monstrous ranch.

Behind the enclosure was a veritable town. Smoke issued from the open doors of an adobe blacksmith shop in which two forges were going, their bellows worked by Mexican boys. In one of the smaller, walled corrals, a couple of men were breaking horses. Before a huge storehouse, several more men were unloading a train of freight wagons.

Like a town, there was an even street on both sides of which were the adobe houses in which the Mexican families lived. A bunkhouse large enough for fifty men, a cookshack, barns. And pigs and chickens everywhere.

But he fell into the routine of the ranch with surprising ease, due probably to Profitt's help. He rode with Profitt for the first few days, and with a man called Duke, with another named Romero.

Winter work. Shifting cattle from one part of the range to another. Digging out waterholes. Doctoring sick cattle. Sometimes they didn't get in at all for the night, but stayed out under the stars and arose before dawn lightened the sky so that they would be finished eating breakfast and ready to ride by the time it was light enough.

Twenty a month and keep — more money than he had ever earned in his life. First payday he watched the house until he saw Dolly come out the back door then hurried to her.

Her eyes brightened when she saw him. Her face flushed with pleasure and she smiled. He took her hand

and dropped the two coins into it. "Keep it for us. To get married on."

He saw the tears spring to her eyes. He reached for her and she fled into his arms. On the point of lowering his lips to hers, he suddenly realized that they were not alone. Leonard Goodwin had come around the side of the house and was watching them.

Clay crushed her against him, whispering, "Leonard. He's standing over there."

He released her, waited while Leonard approached. Leonard's eyes were wicked. "Brother an' sister? Like hell you are. I'm goin' to do a little checkin' on my own. Write some letters maybe. You lie about a thing like that an' it's because you got something to hide. Maybe there's a rope waitin' for you somewhere. If there is, I'll find out where."

A familiar tension stiffened Clay but he didn't speak. He stared at Leonard coldly, aware that Diana had come from the back door and was watching him.

Leonard started to speak, but Clay broke in. "Don't push it. Write all the letters you please. Just stay out of my way an' stay away from her."

Dolly broke the tension by walking away. Diana watched her go into the door, an unfathomable look in her eyes. Then she returned her gaze to Clay. "Want some coffee, Clay?"

He nodded. He walked past Leonard to the door. Leonard grumbled something as he passed, but Clay didn't take it up. Next time he fought with Leonard he'd kill him or be killed himself. It was something he felt, and it puzzled him. He didn't understand the

122

animosity between Leonard and himself, but he accepted the fact that it existed.

He went in, following Diana. He sat down at the table and she brought a pot and cup. There was a vague fragrance to her as she poured the cup full, and she leaned too close. "How old are you, Clay?"

"Seventeen."

"What's the matter with Leonard? What happened between you and him?"

Clay shrugged. "We had a fight."

An odd little light grew in Diana's eyes. "What about?"

Clay growled, "Nothin' much?"

"Dolly?"

He nodded. He wished he hadn't come in now. The only reason he had was to break up that thing in the yard. Now there seemed to be something building up here, something unspoken perhaps but definite all the same. A man feels the things that are in a woman's mind.

He gulped the coffee. "I got to go."

"Why?"

"I'm not supposed to be here anyhow."

"Anybody I invite in here is supposed to be here."

"Maybe so." He went to the door.

She said, "Do you like me, Clay?"

"Sure. Why shouldn't I?"

"Enough to take me riding sometime?"

He felt trapped. But he said, "Sure."

He slammed out the door and hurried across the yard.

As soon as he'd saved a little money, he and Dolly had better get out of here. Before something blew sky high. He didn't want to kill Goodwin's son and he didn't want to get involved with his daughter. And right now both appeared to be inevitable.

CHAPTER
FOURTEEN

He walked slowly back to the bunkhouse. Profitt was standing in the shade, smoking a cigar. Clay said, "How about sending me out to one of the line camps?"

Profitt grinned. "Diana got you on the run?"

Clay flushed uncomfortably. He growled, "Her and Leonard. He wants a fight and she wants —"

Profitt's grin widened knowingly.

Clay felt his temper rise. "Damn you."

Profitt chuckled. "All right. Romero's going out to Canyon Creek in the morning. Go along with him."

Clay nodded. "Thanks."

He turned and stared at the house through the wide back gates in the adobe wall. He hated to leave because of Dolly, yet he knew that if he stayed things would become increasingly difficult.

Staying was, even without Diana, difficult enough. Seeing Dolly every day, being near her, he wanted to touch her, to hold her in his arms. Yet he knew that was impossible. He didn't dare destroy their story that they were brother and sister. Not with Leonard trying so hard to find a hangman's noose someplace waiting for Clay.

And so he rode out in the morning without even telling Dolly goodbye.

Romero was a wizened, wiry man in his forties, who wore his blue-black hair long and who had a whitish scar running from temple to jawline. A taciturn, almost sour man, he rode along in silence through the crisp winter sunshine.

Gradually, as they rode, the land raised in series of step-like bluffs each higher than the last. At sundown they rode down into a deep canyon and came upon a tiny cabin built of adobe.

A lonely existence, this. Each day Clay rode out to southward and Romero to the north. Riding along a bluff rim that marked the boundaries of Goodwin's Cross Bar Ranch, Clay would read the ground for tracks and when he found those of cattle crossing over to the east, he would follow and push them back.

He was both lonely for Dolly and lonely for companionship. Romero remained taciturn and uncommunicative. So Clay spent most of his spare time hunting and practicing with his gun.

A month passed, an uneventful month, and then one warm afternoon, Clay spotted a rider coming toward him from the direction of the ranch.

He reined up at the edge of the bluff and watched. The rider came on at a steady lope, a horse-killing gait considering the distance this spot was from the home place.

Excitement leaped in him the instant he saw that the rider was a woman. Dolly! He slid his horse down off the bluff and galloped toward her.

126

But as he drew near, his excitement faded, to be replaced by irritation. The rider wasn't Dolly. It was Diana Goodwin.

She pulled her lathered horse to a halt a dozen feet from him. Her face was dusty, her hair beginning to loosen from its piled-up position atop her head. Her eyes were warmly mocking, her lips full and smiling.

"Did you run away from me?"

"Profitt sent me out here."

"But you asked him to."

"Did he tell you that?"

She laughed. "No. I guessed it."

Clay stared at her uncomfortably. There was a directness about her that was disconcerting.

Clay had matured tremendously in the past months. He had grown taller and had filled out. Still bony and lean, he had hardened and honed down to a fine, sharp edge.

His face was covered with a fine growth of pale, soft whiskers and lines had begun to form around his eyes from squinting against the glare.

He sat his horse loosely, seeming to be almost a part of it. Diana's eyes held a strange expression as she stared at him.

Clay said, "What do you want? Did somebody send you?"

She laughed easily. "You promised to take me for a ride and then went off without doing it."

Clay said, "You mean you came all the way out here —" He stopped. "How the hell do you expect to get back tonight?"

"Who cares if I get back?" She dismounted and tied her horse to a scrubby clump of brush. She went over and sat down on a rock. She stared up at him mockingly.

Clay swung off his horse. "You get back on your horse and go on home. Better still, come along with me to the cabin. I'll get you a fresh one there."

"Let's rest a while."

Clay stood over her, staring angrily down. There was no mistaking the way she was looking at him. He felt an answering fire begin to burn within himself.

She stood up and moved close to him. There was an earthy fragrance about her today that he had never noticed before. She said, meeting his eyes recklessly, "You've never kissed me, Clay. Kiss me now."

Clay wished he were a hundred miles away. He wished he were any place but here. Because he knew suddenly that he wasn't going to run. He was going to take her in his arms and . . .

Later he pulled away, shaken, and got to his feet. There was a sleepy, triumphant look in Diana's eyes. "Now do you like me, Clay?"

He wanted to hit her. He looked away so that she would not see the wish in his eyes. He knew what she was — he had always known. There had been no love in their union, nor had it been the first for her. Only because he was new at the ranch had she pursued him.

He said harshly, "Now what?"

"I'm going home."

"Not alone you're not."

That seemed to please her obscurely, and he understood something else about her. Once having caught him, she would no longer pursue as openly and shamelessly as before. It was his turn now, to wait, and plead, until she would finally allow him another moment like this had been.

Only he would neither wait nor plead. She could go to hell.

He said, "Get on your horse."

She got up. She stood for a moment, piling her hair atop her head and pinning it. Deliberately watching him she straightened and rearranged her clothes. Clay felt his unwilling desire rise again and hated himself for it.

He mounted his horse. Glancing at her, he saw that mocking smile, those knowing eyes. They said as plainly as words could, "You'll come to me. You'll come back now."

But he wouldn't. He repeated, "Get on your horse, damn it. Your father —"

She said, "No one will worry. I often stay out overnight at some line camp or other."

But she mounted her horse and followed him meekly.

They had gone no more then half a dozen miles when Clay saw another rider coming toward them in the distance. He said, "No one will worry, huh? Looks like someone did."

Diana stared at the approaching rider. "It's Sam."

"Sam who?"

"Sam Kemp." Her eyes teased him "*He* wants to marry me. His father owns the place about fifty miles south of here."

"Going to marry him?"

She smiled. "Jealous?"

"No, by God. I wouldn't —"

Her smile didn't waver. "You think that now. But you'll change. You'll think about me at night and you won't be able to sleep. You'll come back to me, Clay. You'll get Luke to bring you in."

He didn't answer. The rider was closer now.

Clay had never seen him before. He judged the man to be almost thirty. A big, powerful man, he was glowering fiercely at both Clay and Diana.

He hauled his horse in, plunging, a dozen feet away. He stared at Diana. "Where the hell have *you* been?"

Clay glanced at her. Her eyes still held that sleepy look and her hair, pinned up so carelessly, had obviously been down only minutes before. Clay felt trapped.

Damn her! Damn her brother! Between the two of them —

Kemp looked at Clay. "You dirty son-of-a-bitch!"

Diana said sharply, "Sam! Stop that!"

"Why? You little trollop, you been rollin' in the grass with him! It's still all over your clothes."

Clay glanced down at his clothes, started to brush at them but stopped himself in time.

Diana said coldly, "You don't own me, Sam."

Kemp was plainly fighting himself. His hand, the right one, was clenching and unclenching inches from the grips of his holstered gun. In another moment, if Diana taunted this man any further . . .

Clay heard his own voice. "You can go home with him. I'm going back."

He reined his horse around. Kemp's voice was harshly intemperate. "Wait a minute, you bastard! I ain't finished with you."

Behind him, Clay heard a brief flurry of movement. He glanced around, a strange tension in all his muscles. In the smallest part of a second now, his gun would be in his hand, smoke billowing from its muzzle.

But Diana had crowded her horse between him and Kemp, and now she screamed, "Clay! Go on!"

He dug spurs into his horse's sides. Pounding away, he could not get the last expression he had seen in her face out of his tortured mind.

Taut facial muscles, so taut her face had become almost ugly, eyes widened and shining with something that made a chill begin in his spine.

She had wanted to let them fight it out; she had wanted one of them to be killed over her. Why she had stopped it Clay would never know. But he did know one thing — Diana was far more dangerous to him than her brother Leonard could ever be.

At the line camp on Canyon Creek days slipped away. Occasionally a norther howled down across the plain, but gradually, as spring approached, the days grew warmer and the grass began to sprout anew. Cows began to drop their calves, and the yearly roundup of steers to be driven north began.

It was work now, from dawn to dark. Profitt sent a crew out to the line camp and they made their headquarters there. Each day the herd they had gathered grew larger until it was well over five hundred head.

Clay heard nothing from the home place, nothing from either Diana or Dolly.

And confusion tortured him. He dreamed sometimes of Diana, but there was always something of Dolly about her in the dreams. And he began to dream anew of another face, with yellow eyes and a red-faced guerrilla shirt. Always in this dream the man was dead until Clay bent to open one of his eyes with a thumb and forefinger. Expecting to find them blue. But they never were. Yellow — and alive.

The man would spring up and Clay's hand would streak for his gun only to find the holster empty. Here the dream would end and Clay would wake, cold, soaked with sweat and filled with a vague kind of terror he had never experienced before. It was as though his mind were endowing the guerrilla with a superhuman quality he could not combat.

But the day did come when Clay and Romero and the others pushed the herd they had gathered in toward the home place to be trail branded and, along with half a dozen other herds, pushed north along the trail.

Many changes were evident at the ranch from the moment Clay arrived. Goodwin was ill and had been so for several weeks. It was shocking to see him gaunt and thin, stooped and frail, scarcely more than a shadow of the man he had been when Clay had seen him last.

In Dolly, Clay saw change too, but one he liked. A new gentleness was in her face and eyes. She spent most of her time now with Goodwin, caring for him as a daughter might, as Diana never would. She greeted Clay with shining eyes and lips parted in a hesitant smile. But a cloud was in her eyes, and Clay wondered guiltily what Diana had said to her.

There was nothing he could explain, nor did he get a chance to try, for he never could manage to be with Dolly alone.

The changes did not end with Goodwin and Dolly. Profitt had changed too. Something about the way he looked at Dolly, something about the way his eyes smoldered whenever he looked at Clay. Profitt was in love with her too, and had come to dislike Clay for hurting her. At least this was Clay's guess, and it fitted the attitudes of both of them.

Depressing changes. Leonard was almost congenial, but Clay knew he could trust this mood in the man no more than he had trusted him before. Winter had only given Leonard's senseless hatred time to cool and solidify. From now on his actions would be planned and calculated — far more dangerous than his old, hot hatred had been.

And Kemp, who would accompany the drive as his father's representative, watched Clay constantly, particularly when Diana was anywhere around.

Diana was the constant one. Her eyes were still hungry, though not as mocking now. Clay had not come to her as she had predicted he would.

For the first time, Clay began to realize how impossible the situation here at Goodwin's Cross Bar Ranch had become. Somehow he and Dolly had to get away and put all this behind. If they did not, they would both surely be destroyed.

He would begin by going along on the drive. Perhaps while he was in Kansas he could find a place for them there.

But there was another reason why he knew he had to go. He had to end his dreams of the guerrilla who had killed his father in the Lawrence raid. He had to find the man if he could. Only after he had done so could he live in peace with himself again.

CHAPTER
FIFTEEN

And so the branding began, a monumental task, a nightmare of dust and sweat, of bawling steers and galloping, lathered, stinking horses, of whistling ropes, of woodsmoke from the branding fires. Three thousand steers, not one of them less than four years old. The span of some of their horns was the height of a man.

Men worked in teams. One would rope the head, the other a hind leg. Their horses, pulling against each other, would dump the ponderous beasts to the ground.

And the branders moved in with their smoking irons. The smell of burning flesh and hair — dust, sweat, aching muscles and bruised bodies.

Crews came from neighboring ranches for a hundred miles around. Their contributions to the herd ranged from fifty to several hundred head.

Brand three hundred a day. Three hundred. The men's faces were gray with dust, their eyes red and rimmed with mud composed of dust and moisture from their eyes. Their teeth flashed in their sun-blackened faces. You could smell every one of them a dozen yards away if your own nose wasn't too used to the smell.

Clay forgot Diana, forgot Dolly, forgot the guerrilla with the yellow eyes. Stiff and sore, he rolled out of his bunk in the morning and, stiff and sore, crawled into it each night. Except when he was on night-herding duty. On those nights he could not remember a time when he wasn't as exhausted as he was now.

Inevitably tempers grew short. The first day of branding there were no fights. On the fifth, there were nine, one of them a gunfight in which a man was shot through the thigh.

And Profitt was everywhere. He wore out a dozen horses a day. He'd rope and drag a man out of a fight, or he'd pistolwhip him to stop it if he must.

Clay worked silently, dully, automatically and without thought. He was a good hand now, adept with a rope, as good a rider as any man in the crew. He ignored the smoldering looks he got from both Leonard and Kemp, ignored the fact that Profitt was curt with him.

There was an excitement about it though — looking out in the morning across the stirring herd, thinking perhaps what a monumental task it was and forced to admire men with guts enough to undertake it.

Clay sidestepped half a dozen fights. He *had* to go to Kansas and would do nothing that might deprive him of that chance. Profitt was edgy, and Clay was still on trial. It wouldn't take much to make Profitt leave him behind.

At last came the evening when the last steer was branded and the job was done. A night when a man could bathe the stink off himself and put on clean

136

clothes. A time of relaxation. A few got drunk but most were content to just let themselves go loose.

Out on the plain the great herd slumbered and stirred, their sound the lowest of rumbling sounds, like distant thunder below the far horizons.

Washed, shaved for the first time, Clay walked toward the house in the first full dark of evening. Self-conscious and scared, he knocked at the door and waited.

It opened and a fat Mexican woman stood staring at him. Clay said, "Dolly. I want to see Dolly."

He saw her then, beyond the bulk of the woman in the door, her head turned at the sound of his voice.

She came out and closed the door behind. He said, "I haven't seen you much. You're pretty in that dress."

"Thank you." A strain between them — a strain his own guilty memory of Diana explained. He said, "I'm going on the drive."

"I know." There was a certain coolness about the way she spoke.

He said stubbornly, "Dolly, I haven't changed. I still —"

"What about Diana, Clay?"

He would feel like a fool and sound like a liar if he told her how it had really been. He said, "I don't want Diana. I want you. It's always been that way. It always will."

Looking at her in the softest of light cast upon her face by the twinkling stars, he felt an ache in himself, a need for her that would never diminish or go away. He had no thought of what she had been before he found

137

her. He knew this girl, knew what she could do and what she could not.

She had changed. She had softened and matured. Giving of herself in caring for the ailing Goodwin had changed her from a girl into a woman grown. Or perhaps it had been something else — hurt because she knew what had happened between him and Diana. Hurt because Diana had not been able to resist taking Dolly into her triumphant confidence.

Anger grew in Clay, unreasonable anger that he could recognize as such, but anger just the same. It pushed them apart, like something tangible between them. He said, "Damn it, I'm a man. Never was a man that couldn't make a mistake. Even you —" He stopped, knowing he had gone farther than he intended.

Her voice was steady and soft. "Not since I've known you, Clay."

He said, "Profitt," and stopped. He'd said it but he didn't believe it. Now he'd have given anything to take back the word and the thought that had been behind it. He said quickly, "I didn't mean that."

For a long time Dolly didn't speak. In spite of the strangeness and hostility that lay between them, there was something else, a current flowing, almost drawing them together.

Dolly said, "Don't go on the drive, Clay."

"I've got to go."

"Why?"

"You know why. I've got to find that Quantrill man."

"And when you have, if you ever do?"

"I'll kill him. Then I'll come back." Odd the way he changed when he thought of the raider. He seemed to be in another place, another time, and not here with Dolly at all. And he was in another place. He was back in Lawrence with the summer sun shining brightly down. He was standing out in the street staring at Quantrill's men crossing it three blocks up, like a parade. He was hearing the shots, like firecrackers in the distance.

And he was regaining consciousness, his face in the dew-wet grass. He was running through the smoke-filled house and beating out the flames on his clothing and finding Mary, dead by her own hand out beyond the edge of town.

Dolly said, "You won't come back. Goodbye, Clay."

He wanted to kiss her, and if he had things might have been different. But he said, angrily now, "Goodbye, Dolly," and walked away from her.

Only because he was so completely exhausted did he sleep that night. And when the first light streaked westward across the sky, he was in his saddle and the herd was moving out. Riding drag because he was one of the newest men, looking back through the blinding dust at the crowd watching from outside the adobe wall.

Dolly was there, Goodwin with her. He wasn't going, then, and this was Clay's first surprise, half expected because of Goodwin's ailing health. Then he saw the wagon pulling out through the gates, saw the woman on the seat.

A woman on a cattle drive. It was unthinkable. But there she was, and it could be no one but Diana.

For the first time, Clay felt a moment's doubt, almost a chill of premonition that touched his spine and went away. Then he was swallowed up in the dust of the ponderous, slow-moving herd.

Ten-twelve miles a day. Three thousand plodding beasts, half wild, edgy from being held so long on the branding ground. A dozen men and a woman, and all the explosiveness such a combination can have. And somewhere ahead — Kansas. Vengeance for Clay or a hangman's noose.

Dolly stood beside Frank Goodwin outside the adobe wall and watched them disappear into a cloud of dust more than a hundred feet high. Her eyes were clouded, her mouth somber and trembling.

She wished now that she had sent Clay off with the warmth he'd wanted when he'd come to say goodbye last night. But she hadn't and now it was too late.

Uneasiness prevaded her thoughts. She knew the fierceness that was in Clay. She knew — recognized the strange predisposition for violence that seemed to live with him.

Now he was out there alone, without even Profitt to help him. Diana had boasted that Clay belonged to her, and Profitt had understood the hurt that had appeared in Dolly's face in spite of her efforts not to let it show. He blamed Clay for hurting her.

Dolly understood Diana perhaps better than Diana understood herself. She knew Diana's compulsion for conquest. She knew that Diana deliberately set men against each other and derived some sort of twisted pleasure from their conflict over her. She had seen the way Kemp looked at Clay.

Neither had she missed Leonard's new attitude toward Clay which was, she knew, even more dangerous than his old open hostility had been.

Goodwin stared down into her face. He was thin, and the old robust color was gone from his face. He said, smiling slightly, "He's not your brother, is he, Dolly?"

She shook her head.

"And you're in love with him?"

She nodded.

"Want to tell me about it?"

Her face was paler now with her memories. "The part about the wagon attack is true. Only Clay wasn't there. And it wasn't my parents that I was with."

She went on, "I lived with my stepfather in Indiana. After I started growing up —" She looked away. "I couldn't live there any more. There were some neighbors of ours coming west. They took me with them."

The memories were bitter and frightening, as much so as Clay's must have been, she knew. "They had a cow that broke loose one night and I went out to look for her. When I got back, Indians had been there and left. The bodies were on the ground." She shuddered visibly. "And the wagon had been burned."

"I stayed there for a couple of days because I didn't know where else to go. Finally two men came along and found me. I was — Clay and his friend found me with them." She stared at Goodwin painfully. "Jase and Phil used me for bait. When someone saw me and came into their camp, they'd attack and kill them and take whatever horses and things they had. With Clay it didn't work. His friend panicked but Clay killed both Jase and Phil. It wasn't very long afterward that you found us."

"What's Clay's story? Do you know?"

Dolly stared at him thoughtfully. She felt she could trust him, not only with her own story, but with Clay's as well. She had to trust someone. She had to have help.

"He lived in Lawrence, Kansas. He was there when Quantrill made his raid. Clay's father was killed and his sister had to watch. Clay was wounded, but he got his father's body out of the house and went to look for his sister. When he found her, she had already shot herself."

They were walking back now, slowly, toward the house. "Lance Norton had been engaged to Clay's sister. When he heard about it, he deserted and came home. A Union soldier came after him and Lance killed him. He ran and took Clay with him. At a farmhouse outside of town by several miles, Lance killed another soldier. After that they both came west."

"When did he tell you this?"

"While we were caught in that storm. We thought we were going to die. I'm not even sure he knows how much he told me. Some of it was almost delirious."

142

"And you think if he goes back to Kansas he may be held and tried for those soldiers' deaths?"

"He's sure to be. At least for the second one. He and Lance were together and Lance is dead. Clay thinks they'll consider him equally guilty."

"I'll send a man out and bring him back."

She shook her head. "He wouldn't come. He remembers the face of the man that killed his father. He has nightmares about it. Even if you fired him, he'd go on by himself. It's something he's got to do."

No. Clay would not come back, and even if he would, Dolly wouldn't ask it of him. Perhaps he'd never find the guerrilla he was searching for. But he'd never rest until he tried. Thirst for vengeance had been a part of Clay as long as Dolly had known him. Until he had satisfied, by success or by failure, his need for it, he would never be able to live in peace with himself.

She walked with Goodwin back to the house, left him sitting listlessly in a chair on the gallery. She went inside.

It was not altogether what might happen in Kansas that Dolly feared. It was other things. The explosiveness of Diana's presence on the drive. The hatred borne Clay by both Kemp and Leonard Goodwin. The same cold premonition that Clay had felt suddenly touched Dolly's mind. Twelve men and a woman had started out with the cattle. But not all of them would reach the rails in Kansas alive.

Despair touched Dolly's heart. Clay meant more to her than anything else in the world. And she was completely unable to help him now.

CHAPTER
SIXTEEN

Twelve men and a girl. There was Profitt, ramrodding
the drive. There was Leonard Goodwin and Sam Kemp
and Clay.

Romero rode point, Goodwin and Kemp on the right
flank. The one called Duke rode on the left flank,
together with a youngster named Will Purdue from one
of the ranches east of Canyon Creek.

With Clay in the drag rode a skinny oldster named
Jed Crabb. The remuda was herded along a mile or so
to the left of the herd by Mart Roberts, a reckless-eyed,
dark man of about twenty-five, and by Thor Muller, an
old-timer on the Cross Bar who herded horses because
he preferred them to cattle. Besides these, there was the
cook, Pete Niehaus, and his helper who went simply by
the name of Jude.

Ten-twelve miles a day. Eating dust in the drag until
he tasted it in all his food, until it made his teeth grate
noisily as he slept, rode Clay. His eyes rested somberly
on the northern horizon. The wagon traveled well to
the right, the horse herd to the left. Usually as the
afternoon progressed, the wagon drew ahead and was
there with supper ready when they camped at night.

For a time, Diana kept to herself, apparently well aware that they had not yet gone so far that Profitt couldn't force her to return.

But an explosive situation even without aggravation from Diana. Leonard stared oddly at Clay across the fire at night, an almost fanatical light in his eyes. Kemp glowered openly whenever Clay came near. Profitt was cool — reserved.

A week passed. Two. Three. The drive fell into an efficient daily routine. Nearly three hundred miles lay behind. Tempers, already edgy from the fourteen hours daily put in on roundup and gathering, had not improved by the endless, weary monotony of the drive itself or by the heat, the endless dust.

The younger members of the crew watched Diana across the fire at night and, being Diana, she met their glances with reckless, inviting ones of her own.

At first it was only those looks that could make a man's blood run hot. When either Clay or Kemp caught her at it, her lips would curve into that familiar, mocking smile.

And then, the rain. It began with a slow drizzle on the twenty-second day. By night it had developed into a steady downpour.

Clay hunched miserably in his saddle, cold, wet, but breathing pure air for the first time since the drive began. His horse slipped and slid in the churned-up mire left by the pounding hoofs of three thousand cattle. And fell three times that day when Clay whirled him to chase a bunch-quitting steer.

When he came in that night, he was not in the best of moods, certainly in no mood for Diana.

She met him at the edge of the fire. He glanced at her, then knelt to spread his chilled hands to the blaze.

She said, "Stop avoiding me."

He glanced up, scowling. "Why should I stop? I don't mean anything to you."

"Have I told you that?"

"You don't need to tell me. It's plain enough. No man means anything to you. Not for very long."

Her eyes blazed angrily. Clay stood up and stared at her. He understood her now, understood her and wanted no part of her. Shivering miserably, he stood there soaking in the heat of the fire. His eyes were red-rimmed, his face gaunt from lack of sleep. His horse, covered with mud, stood listlessly a dozen feet away.

Diana moved closer. Her voice was throaty, soft. "I could warm you up."

Clay stared at her coldly. "I'll stay cold. And maybe stay alive."

Her face twisted and her eyes blazed. "You son-of-a-bitch!"

Kemp came riding in with Leonard, dismounted and stepped to the fire. He glared at Diana and then at Clay. He said harshly, "Get away from her!"

Clay shrugged. "Sure." He went to his horse, mounted and rode back out toward the herd. Glancing around, he saw Kemp raging at Diana, Diana raging back.

146

Uneasiness touched him. What he had known would happen had begun. They were far enough from the ranch so that Diana could be sure Profitt wouldn't send her back. He couldn't send her alone through Comanche country and he couldn't spare men for a guard.

Clay didn't know why Diana seemed to enjoy taunting Kemp. Perhaps because Kemp was so jealous and possessive. Perhaps because he was easy to taunt.

She saw him watching her and moved close to Kemp, putting up her hands to touch Kemp's whiskered face. Before Clay turned, he saw Kemp seize her fiercely in his arms and heard Diana laugh.

She was wasting time on Clay. Not that he couldn't remember being with her out near the Canyon Creek line camp. Nor that his blood didn't heat at the thought of repeating it. It was just that now he understood her, understood that she would roll in the grass with any man, any man at all, feeling neither love nor affection nor indeed even liking for him.

Clay rode out to the herd and relieved Will Purdue. It was getting dark. Rain blew across the land in sheets, lying puddled on the ground. It ran down the back of Clay's poncho through a tear in it and soaked him from the waist down. Purdue rode miserably toward camp and Clay slowly circled the herd.

Great, dripping beasts, lumbering to their feet as he materialized out of the driving rain. He began to hum, occasionally singing snatches of some song he knew. When he tired of that he talked softly to himself or to the cattle. Anything to let them know exactly where he was so he'd startle none of them as he rode in sight.

A bad night. They were restless anyway from the storm. He heard Profitt coming, and a few moments later the foreman rode up beside him. Profitt paced along beside him for a while, finally asking, "Everything all right?"

Clay said, "It is here."

"What the hell do you mean by that?"

"I mean it ain't all right in camp. What'd you let her come for anyhow?"

Profitt scowled at him. "Goodwin wants to send her to Chicago for a while. He figured this was easier an' safer for her than traveling to the gulf for a boat."

Clay said, "She's got Kemp ready to come apart."

"You think I don't know that? I been watchin' her. Just you stay away from her and from that hot-headed Kemp, too. Understand?"

Clay nodded. Profitt rode on ahead to check the next night guard. Clay turned and rode back, retracing his path along the eastern rim of the bedded herd.

The sky was velvet now, black and dripping. Wind whistled out of the southeast, driving rain almost horizontally to the ground. Occasionally Clay would hear a dim rumble of distant thunder. He hoped it came no nearer.

Streams, even the inconsequential ones, would be flooded tomorrow and choked with floating snags. The herd would have to swim.

He made half a dozen slow passes up and down the rim of the herd. Occasionally, at one end or the other, he would encounter one of the other guards and sometimes they'd stop and exchange a few low-spoken, grumbling words.

At midnight, Crabb came out and relieved him. He rode gloomily in, thinking of his soaked bed, thinking that tonight he probably wouldn't get warm at all.

He rode to the rope corral and caught himself a fresh horse. Leading him, he walked toward the fire.

He heard the voices first, from some heavy brush off to his right. Diana's and a man's. Then he heard the sucking, noisy sound of a horse plodding through the mud. Immediately after that he heard a startled curse.

He paused, debating the wisdom of interference. He decided against it as he recognized Profitt's voice, angrily cursing, damning both Diana and the man.

A small grin touched the corners of Clay's mouth. She'd got caught this time. He knew he ought to move on but he couldn't. He stood frozen there in the driving rain.

Mart Roberts came shuffling toward him, head down, and went past without even seeing him. There was the sound of a struggle back in the brush, Diana's shrill, "Damn you, get your hands off me! No! Stop it!"

Clay's grin widened gleefully, for he heard another sound, unmistakable and plain. It was the flat of Profitt's hand landing with vicious regularity, accompanied by grunts of anger and exertion from Profitt, accompanied too by Diana's hysterical, furious sobs.

Still grinning, Clay turned and plodded away toward camp. If Diana's father had given her more of what Profitt was giving her now while she was growing up —

He reached the fire and stopped beside it to warm his chilled hands. He stared into the leaping flames.

Suddenly from the direction he had come, he heard an angry shout, neither Profitt's voice nor Diana's. Instantly following it was the sharp, flat sound of a shot, partially muffled by the falling rain.

Startled, the men sleeping beside the fire leaped to their feet. They hit their saddles almost instantly, having looped the reins of their horses around their wrists before they went to sleep.

Clay whirled and swung to the back of his own horse. The others rode furiously toward the herd, which might be startled enough by that shot to stampede. But Clay rode toward the sound of the shot.

It was followed by another. And immediately by Diana's scream.

Damn! If the cattle didn't run from all that noise, they wouldn't run at all tonight.

Clay thundered through the brush. It whipped and slashed his face, showered him with water. He hauled up before Diana and swung to the ground, running.

Profitt was down and so was Kemp. Down in the mud and puddled water, lumped, unrecognizable shapes in the nearly complete darkness.

Clay reached the first, saw it was Kemp, and stumbled on. He reached Profitt and knelt beside him in the mud.

Rain beat into Profitt's face. His eyes were closed. Clay yelled, "Luke! How bad you hurt?"

Luke didn't answer. Awkwardly, Clay slid his arms under Profitt's body and awkwardly fought to his feet.

Staggering under Profitt's weight, slipping and nearly falling half a dozen times in the mud, he stumbled away toward the fire. Reaching it, he laid Profitt on the ground beside it and put his ear to Profitt's chest.

There was heartbeat, but it was faint and irregular. Clay lifted his head and stared into Profitt's face.

It was pale and smudged with mud. Unshaven. Gaunt. Clay fumbled for his knife and slit Profitt's poncho. He saw the blood, then, that had drenched Profitt's shirtfront. Clotted already, the redness glistened in the flickering light from the fire.

With every breath, a light froth bubbled from the hole in Profitt's chest. And seeing it, Clay knew that Profitt didn't have a chance.

A wary man, a careful one, Profitt had lived through a dozen gunfights. Tonight he had probably not even considered the possibility that Kemp would challenge his authority with a gun.

Profitt opened his eyes. His lips moved.

Clay tried to hear, but he could not. Profitt's eyes stared up at him, trying frantically to say what his lips could not. Then, almost reluctantly, they closed. His chest stopped its irregular rise and fall.

Clay stared down in unbelief. Only minutes ago Profitt had been spanking Diana, administering discipline long deferred, and it might have changed things, too, if Kemp hadn't interfered.

Clay stood up. He realized that his eyes were burning, that his throat was tight and choked. He felt much the way he had felt when he saw his father's body lying in the burning kitchen back in Lawrence. And

151

then his anger came — anger because Kemp's stupid jealousy of a worthless woman had brought this on.

Leaving the fire, he strode back in the direction he had come. He found Diana crouched forlornly on the ground beside the body of Kemp.

He shoved her roughly out of the way. He put his hand on Kemp's chest.

It rose and fell strongly. He said harshly, "Where's he hit?"

She didn't answer. She crouched unmoving in the mud, only a vague shadow in the darkness. She was sobbing like a child that has sobbed too long, to the point of exhaustion.

Clay knew he couldn't carry Kemp, so he seized the man beneath his arms and dragged him away toward the fire. Reaching it, he laid him down beside Profitt.

He saw now that the wound was in Kemp's leg. Several inches above the knee, it had apparently shattered his leg bone as it passed on through, for bone splinters showed in the ragged hole it had made emerging from his leg.

Enough to incapacitate him, to cripple him. But not enough to kill, if gangrene didn't start.

Clay's mouth was a thin, cold line. He felt no pity for Kemp. Kemp had killed a man worth ten of the likes of him.

Clay stared bleakly into the fire, wondering what would happen now.

CHAPTER
SEVENTEEN

The entire crew had reacted instinctively upon hearing the shots and Diana's scream. Their first thought had been of the cattle, made uneasy by the storm.

Now they came riding back to the fire, to stare down with shocked eyes at the two forms lying beside it.

Clay walked out to where Diana was and yanked her roughly to her feet. She tried to pull away, so he slapped her on the side of the face. "Get hold of yourself! Kemp's leg is smashed and he's bleeding. Get over there to the fire and act like a woman instead of a bitch in heat!"

He could feel her body stiffen. He had spoken in anger and disgust, but now he realized it was the best thing he could have done. It had roused her anger.

She ran from him furiously and he followed more slowly. In a matter of minutes the trail boss had been killed and now they were out here three hundred miles from nowhere with three thousand cattle and no one capable of taking charge.

In his mind, Clay went over the crew. Leonard, the logical one to take over, was obviously unfit for it. Kemp, who might have managed it except for his insane jealousy, was too badly hurt.

Clay doubted if Romero would do it, though he probably had the ability. Duke was too easy-going, too happy-go-lucky to accept that kind of responsibility.

Will Purdue was too young, too unsure. Mart Roberts had caused the trouble and wouldn't be obeyed. Thor Muller was the only one with a chance of success.

Except that Leonard wouldn't let him do it. Leonard would assume charge, claiming it as his right.

And if he did, the herd wouldn't get to Kansas. In a matter of days there'd be more conflict among the hands than there had been during the entire roundup and drive so far. Leonard wasn't strong enough to make nervous, edgy men, most of them older than he, obey him.

He'd try — and the crew would fall apart — cease to exist as a group working toward the same end. Some of them would probably cut away and leave. Others might try and take a cut of the herd. The few that remained wouldn't be enough.

It startled Clay to realize how much had depended on Profitt. He reached the fire. Except for Jed Crabb, Will Purdue and Romero, who had remained with the restless cattle, and Jude, night-herding the horses, they all were here, Pete Niehaus, Thor Muller, Mart Roberts, Duke, Leonard and Clay. Diana had gone to the wagon for flour sack bandages and returned. She knelt beside Kemp, doing a fearful, awkward job of slitting his pants leg to expose the wound.

She uncovered it, stared down trembling for a moment, then got up and ran for the shadows. Clay

154

heard her retching out there and cursed softly under his breath. He squatted beside Kemp and stared at the ugly wound.

It was bleeding profusely, but the bleeding was steady and not in spurts, which told Clay no arteries had been cut. Bone splinters were whitish refuse in the ragged wound. Thor Muller growled in his heavy Scandinavian accent, "He'll never walk again. He be damn lucky to live."

Leonard's voice was unsteady. "Don't stand around looking at him. Somebody fix him up."

All the men stared at Leonard, reluctance to accept his orders plain in their dirty, unshaven faces. At last Thor Muller came heavily around the fire and squatted beside Clay. "We take it off or he dies. Leg bone — shattered like that — it poison him. We got to take it off or let him die."

Clay asked, "You know how?"

Muller nodded. "If I ain't forgot. It been damn long time. You got to cut careful, so not cut artery. When you find, you tie with strings of rawhide. Cut bone back some, then sear whole thing like brand."

Clay said, "Will you do it?"

Muller shrugged. "Guess so. Put him in wagon. You hold torch. Get couple more to hold him down."

Leonard yelled, "Wait a minute, by God! Sam's a friend of mine. Nobody's goin' to hack off his leg while I'm around."

Clay looked up coldly. "You got a better idea — like lettin' him die maybe?"

Leonard's eyes pinched down. His mouth tightened and some of the color left his face. He said, "You ain't goin' to touch him!"

It would have come; it had been inevitable. Clay owed something to Profitt and to the elder Goodwin too. He owed them his life and Dolly's life, and a debt like that can never be repaid in full. But a man can try and do his best, and Clay meant to do that now. He said, speaking past Leonard to the others beyond, "A couple of you pick him up and put him in the wagon. We're not going to stand here and watch him die."

Leonard shouted, "No! Don't a damn one of you move!"

The old familiar tension was suddenly strong in Clay, but even as he stood there waiting for Leonard to move, he could realize that this wasn't over Kemp at all. It had begun a long, long time ago, when Clay and Dolly had first been found. It had steadily marched to this place, this time, and now it would be settled once and for all.

He took a steady step toward Leonard without sacrificing his readiness, his balance, his alert watchfulness. He said evenly, "You move your hand, Leonard, and I'll blow your head off."

Leonard's body was like a tightly coiled spring. His eyes were slits, reflecting the red light from the fire. Rain dropped softly now upon the men, upon the fire, hissing sometimes as it struck a red-hot coal. It was a sound, too, out there in the night, a soft, murmuring sound like a slow-moving stream rolling along in its bed, like the Kaw River on a summer's day.

156

But there was no sound from the men — no sound of movement, no sound of breathing. Only the fire and the rain.

Clay took another steady step, knowing he was a fool. He should stand his ground and kill Leonard the instant his hand streaked for his gun.

The obligation again — part payment for his life, for Dolly's too. Leonard was Goodwin's son.

Leonard's eyes seemed to pinch down a little more with each short step Clay took. In a moment now . . .

He saw the spasmodic tightening of Leonard's body and knew it for the beginning of his draw. His hand was on the grips of his gun and it was slipping out with blurred speed, but he wasn't standing still. He was moving forward, closing with Leonard and knowing he was foolish for doing it, knowing it would probably cost him his life.

His gun was up, cocked. He could have shot at any time. But he didn't shoot. Instead he raised the gun, higher, higher, and when he was but a yard from Leonard, brought it down in a savage, chopping motion. It struck Leonard's forearm as his gun leveled and spit flame and smoke.

The smallest part of a second between the fastest draw and the slowest one. Leonard's bullet plowed a furrow in the mud, made a sound striking like the sharp slap of a hand. Without stopping the swing of his gun, Clay brought it around in a wide arc and up, so that its barrel raked Leonard across the forehead above the eyes, cutting deeply, releasing a flood of scarlet blood that spilled down almost at once into his eyes.

A swipe with a sleeve at the gushing blood to clear his vision, and then Leonard was raising his gun again, held in both hands now because his right arm was numb.

Clay poked the barrel of his gun savagely into Leonard's belly and as the man doubled involuntarily forward, clipped him on the top of the head. Leonard folded forward, his gun firing a second time from the nervous tightening of his trigger finger.

Face down in the mud he lay, trying to turn and roll. Cold, ruthless anger took hold of Clay. He knew what he was going to do. He was going to take this herd to Abilene and kill every man that opposed him. Only complete ruthlessness would enforce respect here now. He drew back a boot and kicked Leonard solidly in the side of the head.

Leonard's face slid along in the mud. His gun was still clutched tight in an outstretched hand. Clay kicked it out.

He repeated in as even a voice as he could manage, "A couple of you pick Kemp up and put him in the wagon."

Diana came stumbling toward the fire. Her face was ghastly, her clothing covered with mud. Her red hair hung loose across her face and she brushed it aside wildly. She rushed at Clay, screaming incoherently.

Clawing, grappling, he slapped the side of her face hard enough to rock her back on her heels, his attention divided between her and the men standing before the fire.

158

Mart Roberts particularly. The reckless light was gone from Roberts' eyes, replaced by sudden, crazy fury.

Sickness in the pit of Clay's stomach. Because one look at Roberts' face told him that now — in a few short seconds — another man must die for Diana. For nothing. For no good reason at all.

This one was too far away to subdue with his gun barrel the way he had with Leonard. This one would have to be shot.

Roberts' high yell, "Damn you, you — !" And the hand streaking for his gun.

Clay's hand hung down at his side, the gun held loosely in its grip. Slower to raise than to draw.

Muscles and nerves jerked tight. The gun came up, thumb hooked over the hammer.

Firelight gleamed redly from Roberts' eyes. Their guns roared out as nearly in unison as the human ear can detect.

An iron seared along Clay's ribs. But Roberts was driven back as though struck by the hoofs of a horse.

Flat on his back in the mud, unmoving. Clay's voice rose with raw, cold anger. "Damn you, pick Kemp up and put him in the wagon! Or do I have to shoot somebody else first?"

They moved at last, like men coming out of a trance, clumsy with haste. Clay was the new trail boss.

They lifted Kemp and carried him to the wagon out there in the dripping darkness. Clay walked over to Roberts. This one — and Diana — were the ones directly responsible for Profitt's death, for Kemp's crippling injury. He watched Roberts' chest carefully for movement, but saw none. Roberts was dead.

Coldly furious, he turned to face Diana. "You're going home. You'll take the wagon and Leonard and Kemp, and leave as soon as it's light."

He heard Muller call from the wagon. He swung to face the men. "Get in the wagon and help Muller hold Kemp down."

They obeyed unhesitatingly. They would have challenged his authority every chance they got, but he knew it was a relief to them to have authority established so solidly. It restored their confidence.

He had no experience and had never been over the trail. He would have to draw heavily upon those who had for what knowledge he needed. They were able men, all of them, or Profitt would not have chosen them for the drive. If Clay could hold them together, make them work together without fighting among themselves, he could get to Kansas with the herd. But not with Diana or Leonard along.

Inside the wagon he held the torch and watched as Muller removed Kemp's leg. He shuddered slightly as Muller tossed it out on the muddy ground. He winced as Muller applied the hot branding iron to the bleeding stump.

Sickened, he went out and stared into the dripping night. He had seven men — Muller, Duke, Romero, Will Purdue, Jed Crabb, Pete Niehaus and Jude. It wasn't enough, but he'd have to make it do. Somehow or other he'd have to make it do.

Scared and worried, he rode all the rest of the night, circling the herd, checking those in camp, afraid to go to sleep as long as Leonard and Diana remained. Daylight brought cessation of the rain and a sun that made the land begin to steam.

Clay watched the wagon head south, leaving deep twin tracks in the soggy ground. Diana drove, and Leonard, still white and sick, rode horseback beside it. They were heading home, but Clay couldn't rid himself of the feeling that the trouble they had caused was not leaving with them.

That morning he gained another member for his crew, a puncher from down on the Brazos who had stayed the winter in Abilene and met them as he was returning home.

Though he agreed to sign on, this one brought him more bad news. "You're headin' into trouble whether you know you are or not. Remember that Jayhawk gang you tied into last year? Well, one of the three you killed was Frank Russell, brother of Jess Russell, boss man of the gang."

Suddenly, vividly, Clay was remembering that night, was remembering too the resemblance one of those killed had borne to the man he sought.

His voice was strange as he asked, "What's this Russell look like?"

"Big bearded man with a face like a hawk's. And eyes a man could *never* forget."

"Why not?" Clay's body suddenly stiffened.

"Color of 'em. Damn near yellow, they are."

Tension ran out of Clay like water running out of a pail. There could be no doubt that Russell was the man he sought. Better still, Russell was also seeking him.

Now, as Clay rode through the blistering, dusty days, there was a strange new look in his blackened, gaunt face. Over and over he relived that day in Lawrence, until it seemed a reality that had happened but a few short days ago.

Hovering always in the back of his mind was a face, a face that had a name at last. Yellow eyes above a thin, cruel mouth half hidden by a heavy beard, brilliant facing on a drab guerrilla shirt . . .

A few more weeks and he'd meet Jess Russell face to face. And he'd kill him, even if he was killed himself.

CHAPTER
EIGHTEEN

As she drove the jolting wagon south, there was little about Diana Goodwin that resembled the woman Clay had first seen standing on the long, shaded gallery of the Goodwin ranch.

Her hair was tangled and uncombed, hanging loosely down her back. Her face was smudged with mud, and lean, sometimes almost ugly. Her clothes were torn and muddy, but she didn't seem to care.

She sat on the hard seat, hunched forward a little, a burning, virulent look in her eyes. Her mouth was compressed, her jaws clenched.

Back in the wagon, Kemp sometimes moaned or cried out with pain, but Diana didn't slack the horses' pace. Nor did she look at Leonard, riding twenty feet to her left.

Her eyes smoldered. Occasionally she glanced back, and when the herd had disappeared from sight into a depression in the land, she yanked the team to a halt.

Leonard rode to her, studying her apprehensively. "What're you stoppin' for?"

Diana stared at him broodingly until he looked away uneasily. He insisted, "Well, why are you?"

Her voice was low. "We're not going home."

"That's crazy talk. What's the matter with you anyway?"

"We're not going home. We're going to Abilene. You can't kill that son-of-a-bitch, and neither can I, but there's someone in Abilene who can."

"I don't know what the hell you're talking about."

"Those men, the ones who tried to rob you and Dad last fall. You didn't kill them all, so some of them got back to Kansas. If we could beat the herd to Abilene —"

Leonard began to grin. Doing so stretched the lacerations on his forehead and he winced. But his grin didn't fade.

He glanced toward the back of the wagon. "What about him?"

"What about him? It's no farther to Abilene than it is back home."

"We'll have to go pretty fast. It ain't going to be easy on him."

Her face was cold, her eyes bitter. "Do you think I care about that?"

He said, "Turn the wagon around and let's go."

Diana slapped the backs of the team with the reins. She turned the wagon and headed northeast, quartering away from the course the herd had taken. She didn't know how she was going to find the town, but she guessed if she kept to the east of the herd she couldn't very well miss it. Sooner or later she'd cross the railroad tracks and when she did, she could follow them on west into Abilene. She recklessly whipped up the horses and behind her Kemp screamed with pain.

164

Leonard dropped behind, an expression on his face now that matched the one Diana wore. Clay Fox might be lightning with a gun, but that wasn't going to help him now.

The days and the miles fell slowly behind. In spite of the slowness of wagon travel, they traveled double the miles covered by the herd and so drew rapidly ahead.

Kemp was in a coma much of the time now. Diana wished he would die. Then she wouldn't have to listen to his groans. She wouldn't have to worry about getting food into him and she wouldn't have to clean up after him all the time.

Traveling in hub-deep mud, through swollen streams and later through heat and blinding dust again did nothing to improve either Diana's appearance or her disposition.

And a little more each day, she grew to hate Sam Kemp. The bandages on his leg had not been changed since the crude operation performed by Thor Muller and Diana did not intend to change them now, in spite of the fact that the stump was rotten with infection and had an almost unbearable stench.

Her patience wearing thin, she stopped trying to feed Kemp, stopped giving him water, even, except when she had to in order to stop his groans.

A day out of Abilene he died and, since they had no shovel, Leonard dumped him in a gully. Next morning, early, they crossed the railroad tracks.

At the first stream thereafter, Diana halted the wagon. She stripped off all her clothes and bathed in the trickle. She put on clean clothes from the trunk in the wagon and made Leonard drive while she brushed endlessly at her waist-length, copper hair. When they drove into the dusty streets of the town, she was again the Diana she had been at the ranch in Texas. Except for a new and not unattractive thinness about her face. Except for the gleam of hatred never absent long from her brooding eyes.

Giving Leonard nearly all the money she had left, she sent him out to make the rounds of the saloons and went to The Drovers Cottage to wait. She didn't have to tell Leonard what to do. She didn't have to tell him a thing.

Knowing him better than he knew himself, she could predict his behavior with unerring accuracy. He'd get drunk as quickly and thoroughly as he could. Drunk, he'd talk, every place he went. Diana was calmly sure that he'd talk about the things she wanted him to talk about — Clay Fox, the herd now hardly more than a week's travel south of town, his hatred for Clay, Clay's uncanny speed with a gun, and the fact that Clay had killed two of the Jayhawkers who had attacked the Goodwin party the previous year.

If he drank enough and talked enough, sooner or later what he was saying would reach the ears of the ones Diana wanted to reach. And Clay Fox's death would be assured.

He was a big man — six feet one even when he wasn't wearing the fancy Texas boots. Bearded, he kept the whiskers trimmed now so that his thin, cruelly twisted mouth was even more apparent than it had been before.

There were deep lines around his eyes, lines that would have told you what he was even if his eyes and mouth had not. A face tanned dark, with a saber scar that still gleamed white along the jawline. A nose that was sharp and hooked like the beak of a hawk, or like the nose of a proud, plains chieftain. And eyes — the eyes that Clay remembered — yellow as those of a prowling prairie wolf, pitiless as those of a snake.

The guerrilla shirt was gone, those days were past. You hid the fact that you had been one of Quantrill's men now. You hid it in Kansas at least, even if you had men with guns at your back.

He sat today in the Applejack Saloon at a table close enough to the bar to hear almost everything that was said.

A man close to Quantrill throughout the war years, Jess Russell knew the value of planning a campaign. Knowledge meant power and knowledge meant success. He knew what herds were bunched on the grass outside of town, waiting their turns at the loading pens. He knew how many cattle each cowman had in his herd, and when they were sold knew within an hour how much they had brought, how much of the money had been paid in cash.

Usually he knew what herds were due to arrive within the coming week. And when a cattleman checked out of his hotel to head back south, Russell knew that too.

Leonard Goodwin was, when he staggered into the Applejack, a familiar type to Russell, obviously the son of one of the Texas cattlemen.

Arrogant, loud, bragging. There was no mistaking this one for a trail hand. Nor was it possible to mistake him for a cowman who had bossed a drive.

Russell poured himself a drink and stared at Leonard's back. Leonard shouted for a bottle and glass and rang a gold eagle on the bar. The bartender brought a bottle and glass and poured him a drink. "Haven't seen you before. Bring a herd north, did you?"

"Part way is all. The damn herd was stole from me."

The bartender clucked sympathetically and Russell listened more closely. Leonard looked around and said in the same loud voice, "Stole, by God, an' the trail boss killed."

"Where'd all this happen?"

"Couple of weeks south of here." Leonard poured himself another drink.

"Jayhawkers?"

"Hell no! One of our own men. One we picked up half froze on the prairie last year when we was headin' home." Leonard stuck his hand condescendingly across the bar. "Goodwin's my name. Leonard Goodwin."

The bartender took the hand. His eyes went to Russell, then flicked away.

Russell's hand had stopped, holding the glass halfway to his mouth. His eyes had narrowed and every nerve, every muscle in his body had gone tight as the skin of an Indian drum.

He got up and walked slowly, easily, to the bar. He grinned at Leonard. "Hear you had some bad luck. Too bad."

Leonard blinked at him owlishly. He grumbled, "The son-of-a-bitch! I'll get him if it takes me the rest of my life!"

Russell asked harshly, "Where's he takin' the herd?"

"He's comin' here."

"Got a lot of brass, ain't he?"

Leonard nodded. "He's a fast man with a gun. Fastest I ever seen."

"That how he killed them Jayhawkers that jumped your party last fall?"

Leonard nodded, thought that over for a few moments and then asked suspiciously, "How'd you know about that?"

Russell laughed. "Everybody knows about that. Three of the men that jumped you came back here. One of 'em was shot up pretty bad."

The explanation seemed to satisfy Leonard, who was now too drunk to think very straight. Russell said, "Let me buy you a drink."

Leonard grinned at him. "You look like a good scout. You just lemme buy you one."

"All right. But I'll buy the next."

Leonard poured him a drink, spilling as much as he got into the glass. He was talking half to himself now, half to Russell. "Hell of a thing, steal a man's herd an' then run him off."

"Where you reckon they are by now?"

Leonard scowled with thought. "We must've made twice the miles they did, an' we been travelin' about nine days. I'd say they was about nine days south. That'd be just over a hundred miles."

"What's he look like, the one that stole your herd?"

Leonard's eyes pinched down and his mouth thinned. "Big. Bony. He ain't as old as me. Blue eyes, or maybe kind of gray. Brown hair, he wears it long. Gun holster stuck down in the front of his belt."

Russell nodded. The description fitted the sketchy one given him by his men last fall. They'd only gotten a brief glimpse and the light had been bad. But this had to be the man.

He said, "Give him a bottle, Jake. On me."

Leonard grinned drunkenly. "Mighty white of you. Mighty god-damn white."

Russell's eyes touched him with contempt. He turned and strode purposefully from the saloon, ignoring Leonard's protesting, "Hey! Don't go 'way. I was just gettin' to like you."

The voice trailed off. Drunk as he was, Russell doubted if Goodwin would even recognize him when he sobered up.

He'd waited for this ever since the first trail herd arrived a month ago. He'd waited, half afraid to hope.

A hundred miles south. If he started today, he could reach them by tomorrow night. He'd have his revenge and their cattle too. As drunk and as stupid as Goodwin was, well, nobody would pay much attention if he was killed in a fight. And if he wasn't here to claim the herd, there'd be no questions asked. Russell could fake a bill of sale. He'd done it successfully often enough before.

Best of all, he'd kill the man who had killed his brother that night last fall.

He realized that he'd forgotten to ask the killer's name. But it didn't matter anyhow. He couldn't miss the herd and the man he wanted would be bossing the drive.

His preparations were both thorough and rapid. An hour after talking to Leonard in the saloon, he was riding out of town, nine men at his back.

Russell could remember the old days, riding with Quantrill. No small groups like this. No worry about the law. They took what they wanted and did what they pleased. And then found safety beyond the Missouri border.

Things were different now. If a man looked closely, he could see the beginning of the end. It was Texas cattle now, beating a hard trail north. But a dozen years from now, the trail herds would be only a memory. The cars that rattled east out of Abilene would carry not Texas cattle but Kansas cattle raised right here on these plains near town.

Soon Russell and his men would have to think about moving west. To the gold camps maybe. He'd heard that robbing miners was even easier than robbing cattlemen. Miners weren't so damned good with their guns.

He shrugged and then his eyes turned hard. He was going to enjoy this raid because there was a personal reward in it for him he had not found in others that had gone before.

He hoped the one he was hunting didn't die too soon. He'd like to make his dying as slow and as painful as he could.

CHAPTER
NINETEEN

They came North by a roundabout way, but one which the ailing Goodwin could stand. East by buggy to the Mississippi, north by river steamer, then west by rail to Abilene. Three riders accompanied them to the river but from there Dolly and Goodwin went on alone.

And eighty miles south of Abilene, Jess Russell led another guerrilla raid, this time against the son of the man he had murdered in Lawrence.

They hit the herd at dawn, from downwind so that they could take the cattle by surprise. A fusillade of shots, high rebel yells, ten horsemen galloping with startling suddenness down upon the stirring herd.

Bawling, they lumbered away, gathering speed as they went. They overran young Will Purdue and pounded him into the ground until his remains were scarcely recognizable as those of a man.

Fortunately for Clay and for those that remained, the guard upon the cattle at this time of day was light. Jed Crabb and Purdue were the only ones with the herd. Crabb escaped the stampede and galloped away on the edge of the herd, believing the others would be coming along to help. Muller had left the horse herd momentarily to grab a bite to eat before the drive started for the day, leaving the new man, Dunn, to watch them until he returned.

Clay, when he heard the shots, was hunkered beside the fire finishing the last dregs of his coffee.

He knew instantly that he was faced with a choice, one that had to be made without hesitation or delay. Stay with the herd and ride out the stampede or forget the cattle and attack the men who had started it.

Five men was all he had. Five and himself. He knew he could count on neither Crabb nor Purdue returning to camp. Their orders were to stay with the herd.

A personal consideration too. He could not help the fierce excitement that rose in him. The man leading the attack on the herd *might* be Russell.

If they rode out the stampede, trying to save the cattle, they'd be scattered. Sitting ducks for the raiders. They'd be picked off one by one.

Not much of a choice. No choice at all. The men were mounted and ready, their horses plunging. The cattle made a low thunder as they picked up speed. Luckily for Clay and the others, the herd would miss their camp. Or was it lucky? Perhaps it had been planned that way.

Clay snatched up the reins of his horse and swung to his back. He yelled, "To hell with the herd! Come on with me!"

The dust was blinding, the sun a luminous reddish ball as it lifted above the eastern horizon.

Clay swung around in the saddle of his hard-running horse. He roared, "Stay together! Stay with me!" He knew that was the only chance they had. For a few

174

moments yet the raiders would be scattered. No doubt at all but that they outnumbered Clay and his men; they wouldn't have attacked unless they had.

So get them one by one, the way they were planning to get the drovers.

Dim shapes through the swirling dust. Dim shapes that disappeared, then reappeared, then disappeared again.

Clay reined hard over when he glimpsed a rider on his left. His gun was in his hand, waiting, ready, waiting until he could see well enough to shoot.

The raiders would be pulling up soon, pulling up to regroup and attack the camp, then to gallop along the fringes of the stampeding herd to pick off the drovers they expected to be there.

The rider Clay was trying to intercept materialized out of the choking dust like a ghost, almost directly in front of him. Clay's gun belched smoke and the man swung in his saddle, startled, hit.

His gun came up, bellowed almost in Clay's face. Then the man toppled from his saddle.

His foot caught in the stirrup as he fell. His horse did not slow down but only veered away from Clay and his men. Clay heard the rider's high scream of terror, diminishing as the horse disappeared, dragging his rider in the dust.

Clay's horse leaped the carcass of a steer. Then he was swinging hard over again toward the dim shapes of several more riders and was hearing their yells. They were grouping, pulling up. He thundered past them, overshooting, as they hauled their lathered horses to a halt.

Clay yanked his own horse in, plunging with excitement. His men pulled up too, overshooting him but riding back at once.

The raiders became visible as the wind thinned the blinding cloud of dust, as the herd drew on ahead.

Half a dozen or more hit them now before the group gained in size. With a high yell, Clay sank spurs into his horse's sides, and the horse plunged back toward the shapes of riders a hundred yards away.

Clay was firing. When his revolver was empty, he shoved it back into its holster and yanked his rifle from the boot.

One of the raiders went down. Behind Clay a man shouted with pain. He yanked his head around, saw but three behind him now. And five remained ahead.

Then he was in the midst of them. He swung his rifle, leaning far out of the saddle to clip a man solidly in the face with its iron-shod butt.

Startled, demoralized, they had expected no attack from the drovers. They had expected Clay and his men to try and save the herd.

Another of Clay's men went down, his throat streaming blood. Two men and Clay remained. Romero and Muller. Muller was standing in his stirrups swinging an empty rifle by its barrel like a club. His face was wild, his teeth gleaming white against his sun and dust blackened face. Glancing around, Clay saw Romero throw a knife. It turned over and over in the air, then buried itself in one of the raiders' bellies, doubling him almost the way a fist might have done.

Three of the raiders were left now. Only three, of this group at least. How many more there were Clay didn't know and wouldn't know until they arrived.

With the last bullet in his rifle, he shot one of them through the throat, then slammed his horse hard against a second, swinging his rifle like a club. Muller had roped the last of the three, dumped the man from the saddle, and was now dragging him at a hard run off toward the place where their camp had been. But he turned and came back, still dragging the man, as a fusillade of shots announced the arrival of several more of the raiders.

Clay counted them as they materialized out of the swirling dust. Three. And one of them, one of them wore a beard and was big enough to be —

With frantic haste he leaped from his horse. Both of his guns were empty but perhaps one of the dead raiders had a weapon that was partially loaded at least.

A hundred yards, fifty, the raiders swept down upon him. Muller was trying clumsily to reload, but it was obvious that he wouldn't make it in time. Romero released his rope, but he had no weapon now with which to fight.

Clay reached one of the downed raiders. The man had a gun in his outstretched hand. Clay seized it, glanced down quickly at its loads.

Three had been fired; two remained. He stood up, waiting spread-legged for the raiders to come within sure range.

A bullet kicked up dust a dozen feet behind him, another squarely at his feet. A third ticked his sleeve, searing along his forearm muscles like an iron.

He could see the bearded one clearly now and it seemed for an instant that he was back on the lawn in Lawrence watching them swing around the corner and gallop toward him. There could be no doubt. The beard was shorter now, trimmed closer to the jaws. But the teeth gleamed white against the darkened face and the yellow eyes glinted.

Clay fired from hip level, touched once again by the same youthful panic that had touched him then. The guerrilla's horse stumbled heavily, fell and somersaulted, throwing his rider clear, throwing him beyond Clay and behind him.

The man struck, rolled, and for a moment disappeared in dust churned up by his rolling horse. Clay ran toward him.

Both Romero and Muller were shooting at last, with weapons either reloaded or taken, as Clay's had been, from the bodies of the raiders they had killed.

Clay had forgotten the others. He could remember only one — the one with the yellow eyes. The one who had killed his father.

He saw the man rising, facing him. Clay's voice was almost a scream. "Remember me? Remember David Fox in Lawrence?" He raised his gun and tightened his finger on the trigger.

But he never pulled it. Something struck him from behind. There was a roaring in his ears, something like an explosion in his head. There was sand and grit in his mouth and the bitter taste of defeat. It had been so close, he had been so close. But he had lost.

Then, for a while, he knew nothing but silence and utter blackness that was like the darkest night.

Dust was still settling slowly when Clay opened his eyes. A wetness was in his hair, along one side of his neck. He put up a hand and found it sticky with blood.

He fought to remember — he didn't know what — and then as it suddenly returned to him, he sat up and looked around.

The bodies of the dead, a few horses standing with trailing reins, Romero and Muller riding toward him from the direction the raiders had gone.

They dismounted and came to him, one of them uncorking a canteen. He drank some water, rinsed his mouth, then said harshly, "Where is he? The one with the beard. Did you get him?"

Muller shook his head. "Got away. He took your horse."

Clay got up. His head pounded fiercely, and he was dizzy enough to stagger. But he could walk and he could ride. He wasn't going to be cheated this time. He wasn't going to lose Russell again.

He walked to one of the raiders' horses and swung to his back. He rode back to Romero and Muller. "See how many of the men you can find. Bury the ones that are dead and help the others all you can. I'll send some men out from Abilene to help round up the herd."

Muller nodded. "You going after them?"

"Him. The one with the beard."

They looked at him strangely but he didn't notice. Hatred was like a burning core in his mind.

He turned away and rode north toward Abilene. And oddly, now, he thought of Lance. Lance should be with him now. Lance had wanted this as much as he.

He was thinking of Mary and of that last evening before the raid. He was recalling the strange closeness that had been between them, closeness never so apparent as it had been that night. Perhaps some sixth sense had told them that death and disaster were close at hand.

He was reliving, too, the morning of the raid — the shock of the bullet, the feel of dew-wet grass in his face, the smoke, the horror of stumbling into the burning house and finding his father's bloody body there.

And later, roaming the town searching for Mary, wandering out beyond its edge. Her weeping, the shot, her last incoherent words.

His face was like granite, his eyes the color of icicles on the north side of a house in winter. He had failed once. He must not fail again.

The herd was gone; the thunder of their going had faded and disappeared. Only dust, a cloud on the horizon, marked the direction they had taken. Clay knew he'd never find them all. But he'd probably be able to gather up all but three or four hundred head. If he lived to gather any at all.

Squinting, he studied the horizon ahead of him, searching for the tell-tale lift of vagrant dust. He saw nothing for a long time, but at last he glimpsed the vaguest stir of dust that was almost instantly gone on the breeze.

He spurred his horse cruelly, forcing the animal into a hard, fast run. If he could overtake Russell before he reached Abilene, his chances would be vastly greater than if he could not.

But as the day dragged on, he began to realize that he wasn't going to accomplish it. Try as he would, he could gain no more than a fraction of a mile on the fleeing trio ahead. The horse he was riding had been pushed south from Abilene without much rest. He was worn out now.

And Russell was riding Clay's horse, caught fresh from the bunch only this morning.

In mid-morning, Clay picked up their tracks and after that contented himself with following them. Russell wouldn't get away from him. With this clear trail for Clay to follow, the man wouldn't stay away from him for long.

Clay rode all that day and stopped when the light failed to the extent that he couldn't see their tracks. He was up at dawn and riding again. And in early afternoon he sighted the town of Abilene in the distance.

Dust rose from half a dozen herds on the grass to the north of town. Riders going to and from the town were dark specks in the distance. A train drawing a long line of cattle cars puffed laboriously east.

Clay's eyes gleamed dangerously. The time he had waited so long for was now at hand.

CHAPTER
TWENTY

The town did not awe Clay as it had many another drover from the isolated cattle country in Texas. Clay had been raised in Lawrence, a larger and more carefully planned community by far. He had seen Denver, where buildings of more than one story were commonplace.

Abilene seemed to be composed chiefly of false-fronted, one-story frame buildings, many of them hastily thrown together and unpainted.

South of the railroad tracks was what seemed to be a separate settlement, even more unplanned than the town itself. The street was crooked, the buildings set at every imaginable angle as a result.

But it was here, in "Texas Town" as it was called, that Clay began his search. Because it was here that the saloons and gambling houses were. He doubted if Russell would be found in the respectable part of town.

His face was gaunt and covered with a grayish layer of dust. His whiskers, which he had been shaving as often as he could, were almost a quarter of an inch long. His eyes were bloodshot from dust and sun and wind.

His arm and the hair on one side of his head were crusted with blood. The clothes he wore were incredibly filthy and stiff with sweat.

But the look in his eyes was unchanged and the heavy revolver, reloaded now, nestled snugly and efficiently in his belt.

He tied his worn-out horse in front of the Alamo after taking time only to water him. He stared at the three sets of double glass doors, then up and down the street warily.

He would find his man; he knew he would. Not on his own terms perhaps. It was possible he wouldn't even see Russell until he felt the impact of Russell's ambush bullet or heard his shot.

In the Alamo he hired seven men, promising them pay when the herd had been sold and sent them riding south to help Muller and Romero gather the scattered cattle. With this done, he began his search for Russell.

His method was thorough and direct, becoming increasingly so as he met with continuing failure. He would stalk into a saloon, stand before the doors and stare around the room. From here, he would move on to the rooms in the rear, tearing open doors, sometimes kicking them open if they happened to be locked.

Protests invariably died under the steady, harsh impact of his eyes. But he did not find his man.

Systematically he searched through Texas Town, not finishing until he had searched each saloon, each garish bagnio room by room, had even searched each dilapidated prostitute's shack.

It was almost midnight when he trudged back to the rail before the Alamo, only to find that his horse had disappeared.

Elation leaped in him at once. His man was here even if he had been unable to find him. He had claimed his horse or sent someone else to claim him.

He paused there, unutterably weary but unwilling to quit, even for the night. Probably Russell was watching him or was having him watched. Any one of the drunken cowhands weaving up and down the street might be Russell's man.

Why, then, hadn't he been shot from ambush? Puzzled, he trudged across the tracks and up into the better part of town.

He heard a woman's cry from the shadows of a long hotel veranda, an oddly familiar voice, and paused. Then he shook his head bemusedly. He had better get some rest. He was hearing things. He'd have sworn that was Dolly's voice.

He turned to go on and then heard it again, along with quickly running feet on the hollow-sounding boardwalk. He whirled, hand going automatically to the grip of his gun.

It was a woman. It *was* Dolly! She flung herself at him in much the same way a lost puppy flings itself at its master. She was weeping with relief — and joy — and her voice was incoherent. "Clay! Oh Clay, I thought I'd never find you! Are you all right? Thank God you are! Clay." She was laughing now and crying too. Her arms around his neck were surprisingly strong, her lips warm and eager, her face wet with tears.

184

"How'd *you* get here? I thought —"

"I was worried. I knew. I thought something might happen to you. I got Mr. Goodwin to bring me. He wanted to see a doctor in St. Louis anyway. We came by river steamer and then west by train. We just got here yesterday. Clay, are you really all right? Is Luke? And the others?"

He said, "They're all dead and the herd's scattered. Muller and Romero are all that're left. And Diana and Leonard and Kemp. I sent them home in the wagon more than a week ago."

"What happened?"

Clay said wearily, "It's a long story. But he's here, Dolly. He's here! I've seen him. He was the one that stampeded the herd and I followed him here."

She gripped his arm. "You look exhausted and you need some rest. Come on. Mr. Goodwin has several rooms. I'll get you something to eat if I have to cook it myself."

He followed her reluctantly. He was beginning to realize that he'd not find Russell until Russell was ready to be found. He had thought — hoped — that Russell would try to ambush him somewhere in one of these dark alleys or streets. Apparently Russell wasn't ready for that. Apparently he had something else in mind.

Dolly chattered incessantly, happily, as they walked. But Clay's mind was only partly on her words. He was thinking, planning. Tomorrow he would try another tack. Tomorrow he'd go down to Texas Town and spend the day in a saloon. He'd get himself roaring drunk. If Russell wanted an advantage, then Clay would give him one. Drunk or sober, he would kill Russell no matter how many bullets the man put into him first.

But tonight he'd eat, and rest. He'd take a bath and put on clean clothes. He'd be with Dolly again.

And he'd think, dream of the way it was going to feel as his bullets tore into Russell's body, as Russell went down before his eyes. He'd promised Mary that and he'd promised himself. He'd even promised Lance.

Through the lobby they went, drawing the curious stares of a few who still had not retired, up to the suite of rooms Goodwin had engaged.

Goodwin was asleep, so they talked in whispers. With Dolly close beside him, Clay related all that had happened on the ill-fated drive. Ending with the attack by Russell and his men, their defeat and the pursuit into Abilene.

Then, even as he talked, Clay's eyes closed, his head drooped and he fell asleep.

Carefully, her eyes warm and soft, Dolly put his feet up on the sofa. She pulled off his boots and covered him. She blew out the lamp and sat in a chair, watching him as he slept.

Again, for Dolly, it was just as it had been out on the plains alone with him. She saw the restless way he stirred as he dreamed. She heard his voice cry out.

But he didn't wake. He slept heavily until the sky began to gray in the east.

CHAPTER
TWENTY-ONE

There was a feeling in Clay when he woke, a strange certainty that this was the day — the day he would find Russell. It was a feeling composed partly of uneasiness, partly of excitement.

Dolly was dozing in the chair. Her eyes were closed, her face a little flushed. Her lips were parted, the rise and fall of her breasts was regular and light.

Without moving, Clay watched her for several long moments. And watching her, he forgot to hate. Instead he felt a tightness in his throat, a hunger and need that was almost an ache in his chest.

He forced himself to look away. If he stayed here he would be talked out of the vengeance he had waited for so long. He would go back to Texas with Dolly. Mary and his father would remain unavenged along with the drovers murdered when Russell stampeded the herd.

Carefully he sat up, carefully got to his feet. She had covered him and removed his boots. Thinking of her doing that for him almost changed his resolve to leave.

But hatred and a burning thirst for revenge had been a part of him too long. He turned away, painfully aware that he might be seeing Dolly for the last time, that he might not live through the day.

Walking carefully, carrying his boots, he went silently to the door. He opened it, eased it shut behind him. Only then did he stoop to put on his boots.

He knew a little now of the man he pursued. Russell was merciless and cruel, but he was also bravest when he had armed men at his back. And Russell liked the odds heavily on his side. It was why he had not stopped and made a stand on the way into Abilene. It was probably why Clay had not found him yesterday.

Yet it was also probable that Russell knew Clay had figured prominently in the killing of his brother last fall. He would know by now that the herd he had stampeded had been Goodwin's herd by reading the brands if in no other way. He may have recognized Clay from descriptions given him by survivors who had returned after the abortive attack last fall.

Eventually Russell would let himself be found or would find Clay. Russell wanted revenge for the death of his brother as badly as Clay wanted revenge for the raid on Lawrence. But it would be on Russell's terms — at a time when he didn't figure he could lose, at a time when he could make Clay's death as painful and prolonged as possible.

Clay hurried out of the hotel and turned immediately south toward Texas Town. The certainly that today would be the day grew in him as he walked. In spite of the brightness and warmth of the Kansas sun, a little chill crawled into his spine and stayed there.

The street was practically deserted. A few horses were still racked before the saloons, drowsing in the morning sun. As Clay walked along, a puncher got up groggily from the weeds and staggered across a tin-can dump to where his horse was racked. He looked at Clay, grinned in a way both sick and apologetic and muttered, "What a night! God what a night. Never again."

Apparently the saloons never closed, for they were still open this morning. Clay went into one of the smaller ones and ordered breakfast. When he had finished, he left and went down the street a few more doors to the Alamo.

The first drink gagged him and so did the second. He wasn't used to drinking and didn't like the taste. Nor was he used to its effects.

He drank slowly but he drank steadily. And as the day progressed, a core of anger grew in his brain. He glowered suspiciously at everyone who came in. Occasionally he got up and staggered toward the free lunch counter to help himself to something to eat. Eating, he had heard, kept a man from getting too damned drunk. He had to be visibly drunk, but if he let himself become incapacitated, he was dead.

In mid-morning, he went out back and, returning, tried drawing his gun. It seemed to him that he was faster than ever, but he realized that he might well be deluding himself. Alcohol produced peculiar hallucinations in a man's mind. It gave some men courage; it made others quarrelsome; to others it gave confidence all out of proportion to their ability.

Noon passed with no sign of Russell or either of the men who had escaped the raid with him. Clay got up and staggered out into the sun, blinking against the glare. His head was beginning to ache. He felt hot and feverish. He felt edgy and anxious and a little mean.

Damn Russell! How much of an advantage did the bastard want? Did he want Clay flat on his back before he'd drum up enough courage to attack him?

Clay began the rounds of the saloons, having a drink in each, helping himself liberally from free lunch counters and trying to do so without seeming obvious about it. In mid-afternoon he put his head down on the table and appeared to go to sleep. But he wasn't asleep. Every nerve in him was tense and his ears picked up every sound.

This way, the afternoon waned. Once, as evening approached, Clay thought the moment had come. A man who appeared to be a stockyards worker tried to pick a fight with him. But the fight was broken up and the man thrown out. Clay went on again.

The sun sank out of sight behind the western plain. The shades of dusk sifted along the dusty streets.

Clay was tiring now, tiring and edgy, and jumpy too. He whirled at every sound behind him. In the saloons he sat with his back to the wall.

They found him in the Applejack — Dolly and Goodwin, obviously in much better health than when Clay had seen him last. Dolly was near hysteria. Tears welled up into her eyes as she saw him.

Pulling Goodwin along by his arm, she hurried to Clay. "Where have you been? We've been looking all day for you!"

Clay stared at her with bleary eyes. He was thoroughly drunk now. He said laboriously, "I'm waitin' for him to show himself, that's what."

"You're drunk. Clay, are you crazy? Are you trying to *let* him kill you?"

Clay muttered, "Couldn't find 'im yestiddy. Figured mebbe this'd bring him out."

Goodwin said, "It'll bring him out all right. But how do you expect to — ?"

Clay said, "I'll get 'im. I'll get 'im before he gets me no matter what."

Dolly pulled him to his feet. "You will not! You're going back to the hotel and sleep this off. You wouldn't have a chance in this condition. Besides that, it isn't only him you'll have to fight. Leonard is in town, bragging that he's going to kill you before Russell does."

"Leonard?" Clay tried to focus his eyes. He realized through the fog hanging over his mind that he had unwittingly done precisely what Russell must have wanted him to do. Russell had been smarter than he thought. The man had seen through Clay's little ruse and had known it for a ruse. He'd waited Clay out, knowing he would get disgusted with the waiting and eventually drink too much.

Clay said solemnly, "All right. I'll go back with you."

Dolly sighed with relief. Some of the terror faded from her eyes. Goodwin said, "Tomorrow I'll help you look, Clay. We'll hire some men. I want him as badly as you do."

Clay nodded. He was tired now, near to exhaustion. His head ached excruciatingly. His eyes were blurred and his arms felt like lead.

With Dolly on one side and Goodwin on the other, he went out the door into the early dusk. Staggering a little, steadied by Dolly and Goodwin, he went up the street.

It came as he had known it would, the bright flare of a shot from the dark shadows behind a building.

Dolly made a small cry and, hearing that, the stupor induced by all he had drunk seemed to evaporate from Clay's mind like a ground mist dissipated by the sun.

He slammed Goodwin aside, heard the man fall against the building wall. Then he was lunging the other way, carrying Dolly with him and down to the ground. If Russell had hit Dolly —

The core of anger in his brain became a fire, consuming him. But his body was cold as ice.

His hand had done its job and the gun was in it, hammer back. But darkness made him blind.

Leaving Dolly in the dust of the street, he lunged to his feet and charged toward the corner of the building. He could see Goodwin coming up, started to yell at him.

Then a gun flared from the other direction, from the direction they had come. He heard Leonard's crazed voice yell, "You son-of-a-bitch! You —"

The gun flared again, and once more Clay flattened himself to the ground.

From against the building wall, Goodwin's gun roared, its tongue of flame pointed toward his son.

192

And three guns flashed at once from the corner of the building.

Clay was rolling, dust kicked up by those bullets filtered into his eyes and mouth. He reached the edge of the boardwalk, and now his gun bucked against his palm. He heard the bullet strike solidly against yielding flesh, making the peculiar smacking noise a man gets to know if he has hunted much.

He charged to his feet again, making it this time to the shelter of the building wall.

But instead of stopping here as they would expect him to do, he charged on to the corner of the dilapidated building and flung himself around it.

He struck the body of a man with a stunning impact, one that rattled his teeth. With a high yell, the man fell back, his gun roaring almost in Clay's face.

Powder stung his skin, but he kept his head. His gun centered with automatic precision and he fired. Again he heard the bullet strike.

There was a sound in the dry weeds. Clay froze, listening. He could hear the sounds of running feet from the street behind him, could hear a querulous shout. His ears pushed these sounds aside, concentrating on that sound in the weeds.

Retreating feet, but not running feet. Russell, having lost his two men, his support, was backing away. Had it been one of the others and not Russell, he would have been running.

Damn the man! Damn him to hell! He was elusive as a ghost! Clay lunged away, running as fast as he had ever run before toward the sound in the weeds.

And the sound stopped. Stopped, faded away into utter silence.

Clay weaved from side to side. He knew there was a little light at his back, a little light in the street. Not much, but enough to dimly outline his running form.

But no shots came. Russell, still playing it safe, refused to reveal his position until he was certain of his target.

Clay fired blindly, hoping that this would make Russell shoot back. But only silence greeted the resounding echoes of his shot.

Clay hated Russell as bitterly as one man can ever hate another. But he did not make the mistake of thinking the man was cowardly. No, backed to the wall, with no other alternative, Russell would fight as courageously as a wolverine. He just liked to stack the odds. He just took no risks he didn't have to take.

Clay's foot stirred a tin can at the edge of a dump. He hauled to a sudden halt. Breathing hard, he listened intently.

He heard nothing, but some sixth sense told him that Russell hadn't gone. The man was here, waiting as silently as a cat.

Clay's nose could almost smell the acrid smoke of a burning town. He could almost hear the distant, popping sounds like firecrackers on the Fourth of July. His mind could see those yellow eyes, those flashing teeth, that brilliantly faced guerrilla shirt.

He said with bitter fury, "Remember David Fox in Lawrence, Russell? That's what I'm going to kill you for. Because I'm his son. I wasn't dead that morning when you shot me down on the lawn. I was alive, and I remembered your face. Now I'm going to kill you, just like you killed him."

All at once he had no more patience with this waiting kind of game. He wanted to see his man; he wanted to use his gun. He wanted to take no chance that Russell might escape again.

One thing only could make that possible. Light.

These dry, dry weeds. They would burn. But how to set them afire without letting himself be seen before he could see the other man?

A chance he'd have to take. He fished in his pocket and found a match. He knelt, carefully gathered dry weeds and grass and placed them in a pile.

Then, huddled over it, he struck his match, laid it in the pile and instantly rolled away.

A gun shouted, and the bullet tore into the blazing pile he had built, scattering flaming bunches of it over a yard-square area.

The second bullet gouged along the muscles of Clay's back as he jerked to his feet.

He could smell the acrid bite of Russell's powder, he was that close to the man. In an instant now . . .

Tense — more so than ever before in his life — he waited, scarcely daring to breathe. That dark shape over there, it could be a man. But his hand didn't move. He'd make no rash mistakes now. He'd wait until he was sure.

The fire grew, and the shape became more plain. At the same instant Clay became sure of his target, Russell saw him and swung his gun the few inches required to cover Clay.

The recoil of Clay's gun against his hand was the most solid, satisfying thing he had ever known. Though he didn't realize it, he punctuated each shot with an almost hysterical yell. "For Pa! For Mary!"

He scarcely felt the bullet that slammed into his arm. He scarcely realized that his gun had fallen to the ground. The fire was blazing now, lighting the whole vacant lot with its orange and eerie glow. Clay stalked to Russell and stared down at him.

The eyes were open still, but the man was dead. With an expression of revulsion, Clay stuck a foot under the body and rolled it over. Shuddering, he turned away. He had waited and planned for this instant, but there was no pleasure in it now that it was here.

But with vengeance behind him, looking toward the street was like looking at a world he had never seen before. Dolly was running toward him through the weeds, unhurt. Goodwin was out in the street, tears streaming down his unshaven cheeks as he knelt beside the body of his son whom he had killed himself.

Dolly stopped while yet a yard away from him. Her eyes were enormous as they studied his face. Her voice was steady and soft. "Is it over, Clay? Have you got room in you for love?"

He nodded dumbly and reached out his arms for her, needing her in this instant as he had never needed anyone before. She came to him with a little cry of joy. For two homeless ones, this was coming home.

ISIS publish a wide range of books in large print, from fiction to biography. Any suggestions for books you would like to see in large print or audio are always welcome. Please send to the Editorial Department at:

ISIS Publishing Limited
7 Centremead
Osney Mead
Oxford OX2 0ES

A full list of titles is available free of charge from:

Ulverscroft Large Print Books Limited

(UK)
The Green
Bradgate Road, Anstey
Leicester LE7 7FU
Tel: (0116) 236 4325

(Australia)
P.O. Box 314
St Leonards
NSW 1590
Tel: (02) 9436 2622

(USA)
P.O. Box 1230
West Seneca
N.Y. 14224-1230
Tel: (716) 674 4270

(Canada)
P.O. Box 80038
Burlington
Ontario L7L 6B1
Tel: (905) 637 8734

(New Zealand)
P.O. Box 456
Feilding
Tel: (06) 323 6828

Details of **ISIS** complete and unabridged audio books are also available from these offices. Alternatively, contact your local library for details of their collection of **ISIS** large print and unabridged audio books.